Horse

Tales

A Carson Reno Mystery

Written by

Gerald W. Darnell

Horse

Tales

Be sure to check out Carson Reno's other Mystery Adventures

Murder in Humboldt

The Price of Beauty in Strawberry Land

Killer Among Us

SUnset 4

Cast of Characters

Carson Reno - Private Detective

Rita - Hostess Starlight Lounge

Marcie – Peabody Hotel Operator

Andy – Bartender Down Under

Mason 'Booker-T' Brown – Head porter Peabody Hotel

Nickie/Ronnie Woodson – Owners Chiefs Motel and Restaurant

Tommy Trubush – carhop Chiefs

Jack Logan – Attorney /Partner

Leroy Epsee – Sheriff Gibson County

Jeff Cole – Deputy Gibson County

Scotty Perry – Deputy Gibson County

Elizabeth Teague – Airline Stewardess and friend of Carson's

Mary Ellen Maxwell – Humboldt Socialite and owner of Maxwell Trucking

Judy Strong – Vice President of Maxwell Trucking

Gerald Wayne – Owner Wayne Knitting Mill

Nuddy – Bartender Humboldt Country Club

Larry Parker – Chief of Detectives Shelby County

Joe Richardson – Associate Drake Detective Agency

Steve Carrollton – Head of Memphis Mafia family

Todd Randal – Trainer *Sugar Creek Farms*

Billy Grayton – Owner *Sugar Creek Farms*

Amanda Grayton – Wife of Billy Grayton

Aaron Nunamaker – Owner *Nunamaker Stables*

Susan Nunamaker – Wife of Aaron Nunamaker

'GetAWay' – Stud horse *'Nunamaker Stables'*

'NharmsWay' – Stud horse *'Nunamaker Stables'*

'AtLarge' – Stud horse *'Sugar Creek Farms'*

'Thunderball' – Stud horse *'Sugar Creek Farms'*

'*Largo*' – Champion Race Horse '*Sugar Creek Farms*'

Dr. Barker – Coroner Gibson County

Bert Sappington – Insurance Investigator

Elliot Farnsworth – Black Diamond insurance client

Eddie Merrick – Jockey and stable worker.

Dr. Jack Preston – Veterinarian

Miguel Rivera – Jockey and stable worker

Justin Avery – Trainer '*Nunamaker Stables*'

Leonard Price – Insurance Investigator

Raymond Griggs – Humboldt Chief of Police

Richard P. 'Dick' Valentine – Former Humboldt Chief of Police

James Henry King – Mafia Associate

Johnie Gibson – Mafia Associate

Sammy 'shiv' Thompson – burglar

Harry Smiley – Jockey

Linda Smiley – Wife of Harry Smiley

Mrs. Theodore Faulkner – Friend of Elliot Farnsworth

Julio Escobar – Columbia Mafia Head

Nathan Crouch – Owner Crouch Motors and Gadsden Speedway

Dedication

To my lovely daughters, Caroline and Stephanie. They never had a horse, but both share my love, respect and appreciation for them.

Contribution Credits

Judy Steele Minnehan

Elizabeth Tillman White

Mary Ann Sizer Fisher

Material Credits

Humboldt Public Library

Gibson County Historical Website

Courier Chronicle

FORWARD

One of Humboldt's well-known horse breeders is brutally murdered, then left to burn in his barn along with his prized stallions. A Jack Logan client has been accused of the murder and Carson has been called in to investigate.

However, getting to the truth is proving to be a real challenge. It seems no one, not even the accused, is capable of telling the truth.

Greed, lust, infidelity, half-truths and the Memphis Mafia all seem to be involved — somehow. Sorting out the pieces and finding the real murderer, will be a monumental task.

Carson becomes involved in the web of lies and faces one of his biggest challenges, as he tries to solve the case of *Horse Tales*.

Chapters

"Life is cheap – make sure you buy enough"

Carson Reno

Introduction

*I*t was a disaster beyond most people's comprehension.

There was nothing left standing of the barn, it had burned completely to the ground. Among the rubble and smoking wood, you could see the smoking corpses - which had once been some of the finest thoroughbred stallions in the Tennessee and Kentucky area.

Unnoticed, among these ruins, were the burned remains of Aaron Nunamaker, owner of '*Nunamaker Stables*', and one of the best known horse breeders and stud farm owners in West Tennessee.

Killing a human being brings the wrath of the law and the accompanying sorrow and grief from loved ones. Killing a helpless animal brings wrath that is unequaled to that associated with killing a person. This sorrow and grief continues long after the grief over human loss has left. Mankind will forget their own losses, but they never forget similar betrayals to animals. Odd isn't it?

The fire had, obviously, been set and was a deliberate murder of innocent animals - horses. Horses, that could not free themselves from their comfortable stable, horses that trusted their caregiver and felt safe in their home. Horses that died a terrible death, and horses that would never know how they became involved in such a terrible scheme and plan.

Tracks reveled that many of the doomed horses had been led from another barn to the one that was burned. This made it more than an act of revenge or rage, but one intended to destroy the animals, all at once, and all at one time.

Other than car and horse tracks, the clues were minimal or non-existent. Police roped off the area and considered it an accident or a rival/revenge act, until they found the body. Then things changed.

He had been shot once at close range with a high powered rifle. The bullet entered his center chest and exited to some unknown parts of the barn or maybe the surrounding ground. His body was burned beyond normal recognition, like the horses, but his engraved Horseshoe ring, which he always wore proudly on his right hand ring finger, made preliminary identification possible.

OAKLAWN

*M*y new associate, Joe Richardson, had a perk I didn't know about. He had his pilot's license and the use of his father's plane, upon request. Joe, along with his date, Marcie (switchboard operator at the Peabody) flew Liz, Jack, Judy and me to Hot Springs for a weekend of horse races at Oaklawn Park.

Liz Teague is a lady friend that I met during a recent client investigation. She is a stewardess with Chicago & Southern Airways and had taken a long weekend. I had put client activities at Drake Detective Agency on hold.

Jack Logan is my lawyer/partner and he had met Judy Strong, Vice President of Maxwell Trucking, during one of our recent cases. Jack just simply cancelled his appointments, and told his secretary to reschedule. We all needed a break, and spending a few days in Hot Springs was a dose of medicine all of us could use.

We were staying at the Arlington, which offered everything a traveler would need. A spa, pool, golf and casino complimented its hotel luxury, and our plan was to relax and play. The Arlington would be our home for the next couple of days.

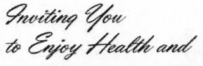

We dropped our bags at the hotel and quickly grabbed a taxi for the track to enjoy our 'day at the races', which was going to start early and end late.

Unfortunately, Jack, Joe nor I were very good at handicapping the ponies. We bet on our horses, tore up our losing tickets and then spent time searching for the bar and discussing the next race, but not Liz. She was cashing winning tickets on every race. Finally I had had enough!

"Okay Liz," I said while tearing up my most recent losing bet ticket. "We surrender. What is your system? What is your trick? How can you have a winner on every race, and we can't have any luck?"

"It is very simple. First, I pick a horse's name I like. Then I pick a jockey's name I like. Then, because I can't decide, I bet on all the horses! See, it worked! I have won every race!"

We all just looked at each other!

I had to say something. "Liz, that is great, but do you win more than you bet? That is the idea, right?"

"No, it isn't," she said raising her head up high. "My idea is to win and have fun, and I'm doing that. What is the problem? Have I done something wrong?"

Judy interrupted. "No, Elizabeth you haven't. The idea is to have fun and winning is fun. So you win and have fun. Forget what these idiots tell you!"

We knew it was best to just let this one go. Liz was having fun, which is what really mattered.

"Okay," Jack said looking at the racing program. "Let's get serious and see if we can pick a winning daily double. Anybody got suggestions?"

Of course it was Liz who had the answer. "Yep, I've already picked them out. We should bet on '*Chili Powder*' in the 9th race and '*MakeNBacon*' in the 10th. Can't miss, they are sure winners!"

"Alright Elizabeth," I laughed. "Please tell us what magical method you used to pick these horses. Why are they sure winners?"

"Because they both remind me of food – and I'm HUNGRY! When do we eat?" She was serious!

"Tell you what," I offered. "You girls go with Joe and Marcie to find us a seat in the Jockey Club. Jack and I will make this 'sure' bet and join you there. Okay?"

They all agreed and hurriedly went in search of the Jockey Club and food. Jack and I fought the huge crowd and finally made our way to the downstairs betting windows.

Waiting in line, Jack pointed to a name he recognized in our racing program. "Do you remember this guy, Todd Randal?" Jack asked. "He's listed as the trainer for '*Sugar Creek Farms*', which is located just outside of Humboldt. They are racing a horse called '*Largo*' in the final 'Stakes Race' today."

"Doesn't ring a bell, why should I remember him?" I didn't recall the name.

"He was a client of mine a couple of years ago. At that time, he worked as a trainer for '*Webster Stables*', which is a breeding and racing business located in Collierville, Tennessee. He got into trouble for some 'questionable' breeding practices, and I defended him on both local and state charges."

"What kind of 'questionable' breeding practices?" I asked.

"False or misleading stud certifications, that kind of stuff, was what he was charged with. He got off with some fines and a temporary license suspension, but it might have been worse. He could have done some serious time."

"Interesting," I said with some interest. "But I really don't understand how all that works; however, I do know there is some serious money to be made when you've got a winning thoroughbred at stud."

"Yes, there is," Jack added. And a lot more money than you could ever make racing a horse. Let's place this bet and then walk down to the paddock. I'd like to say hi to Todd, if we can find him."

We made our 'sure thing' Daily Double bet, and again fought the crowd to find our way to the outside paddock area.

The Paddock had a great view of the horses, jockeys and trainers, but absolutely no view of the actual racing. Jack and I grabbed a drink from an outside bar and watched, as the horses were professionally prepared for their upcoming race.

Eventually, Jack spotted Todd Randal, and made his way over to where he was standing. I held my ground and just enjoyed the excitement of being close to these magnificent animals – they were beautiful! I was also wondering which two were named '*Chili Powder*' and '*MakeNBacon*'. I hoped they were the fast ones!

They finally finished their conversation, and Jack walked back to where I was standing.

"He have any hot tips?" I joked.

"'*Largo*' is the favorite in the stakes race, and Todd said we should put our money on his nose!" Jack said waving his bet money.

"I'm not going to get close enough to touch his nose," I assured Jack. "But, I will bet a couple of dollars with the man in the betting cage when we get back inside. And speaking of inside, we better go find those girls. I'm not sure Joe can handle them for very long."

"Good idea," Jack agreed. "Todd wants to talk later this evening. I told him we were staying at the Arlington, and he's going to stop by after the races."

"Well, I can escort the girls in the casino while you have your meeting. A chaperone for them is never a bad idea," I laughed.

"Nope, he wants to meet with you, too."

"Why?" I frowned.

"I don't know," Jack said shaking his head. "I told him who you were and what you did. Then he asked me to have you join us. I guess we will just have to wait and see what he wants."

Back inside, we made our way through the huge crowd and eventually to the Jockey Club. Joe had the girls seated where they could see the races and Liz was still wheeling her bets and cashing those winning tickets.

JOCKEY CLUB

"Carson?" Liz asked. "Where have you been? We are doing good with our betting, and guess what?"

"What?" I couldn't wait!

"We have already won the first half of the Daily Double! While you guys were off doing, whatever, '*Chili Powder*' won by 4 lengths! And the board says that if '*MakeNBacon*' wins his race, we win $400 dollars! Isn't that terrific?" She was definitely excited.

"Congratulations, I think. Guess we are halfway to being rich – whatever that's worth!" I boasted before realizing that I was spoiling her fun.

"Carson, why are you such a party dud? '*MakeNBacon*' is going to win, and we'll all cheer him on. You'll see," Liz assured.

"What I really need to see is the bartender," I added. "I'll be back in a minute. Anybody need anything?"

I took drink orders and went in search of the closest bar.

The tenth race, the second half of the Daily Double, was exciting. As Liz predicted, '*MakeNBacon*' crossed the finish line first, and it was my pleasure to escort her to the winner's window to collect the money.

We spent the rest of the afternoon in the Jockey Club, enjoying cocktails and a small dinner. But no Chili or Bacon - that I noticed! However, our group did have a very successful day at the track, with winnings unknown, but fun immeasurable.

Marcie, Judy and Liz were looking forward to an evening at the casino, where I expected the Oaklawn money would soon be given to the Arlington. While we were waiting for a cab, I pulled Joe to the side and briefed him about our evening meeting. Until we finished the meeting, he was to be the girl's escort. I trusted him to not let them spend everything on our first night in Hot Springs!

The cab dropped us in front of the Arlington, and we spent the next hour getting ourselves organized in our luxury rooms. The Arlington definitely has excellent accommodations.

Arlington Hotel

It was a beautiful Arkansas evening, warm with a nice gentle breeze and no hint of rain. We gathered in the outside lobby bar at 7, and I quickly sent Joe and the girls off to find the casino. Jack and I planned to join them after our meeting.

Todd Randal arrived promptly at 7:30. I greeted him and shook his hand as he walked up to our table.

"Mr. Randal, my name is Carson Reno. We haven't met, but it's definitely my pleasure. I've never known a real 'horse trainer' before," I laughed and offered him a chair at our table.

"Please call me Todd," he said firmly. "I hope you made a big bet on '*Largo*'. He won the Stakes race going away, the odds weren't great, but I knew he had the field covered."

We had forgotten to do that and I didn't tell him. But, I did know how Liz was betting. "Yes Todd, we did, thanks for the winning tip. Actually our group had a very successful day at the track. They are now in the casino giving it all back, but that's how it works!"

"It's never lucky to hold your winnings too long, bad luck almost always follows good!" he said laughing and adjusting his chair.

Jack sipped his drink before he spoke. "Todd, the last time we met, you were working in Collierville for '*Webster Stables*'. I saw in today's program that you are now associated with '*Sugar Creek Farms*' of Humboldt."

"Yes, and that is what I wanted to talk with you about," Todd looked at us both as he spoke. "I've been working for Billy Grayton for the past year. He is the owner of '*Sugar Creek Farms*' and a very nice man. Not to mention, he is also a very good employer."

"I know Billy Grayton," I interrupted. "Billy and I went to school together, years ago. I'm from Humboldt, in case Jack had not mentioned that."

"He did, and that's one reason I thought it might be a good idea for you to hear my story," Todd said, stirring his freshly delivered drink.

Todd leaned forward and began his story.

There were two major racing and horse breeding operations in the Humboldt area. In addition to his employer, '*Sugar Creek Farms*'; there was also '*Nunamaker Stables*'. For obvious reasons, they were in competition for horse talent and primarily for the breeding opportunities. The money, the real money that is made by these horse-farming operations is not in racing, but in breeding. But, to be successful as a breeder, you had to win races and have the thoroughbred stock to demand and sell stud fees. With the right stock, these fees, and the resulting income from these fees, could be significant. That is really what financed the racing, which just made the whole process one big circle.

'*Nunamaker Stables*' was owned and operated by Aaron and Susan Nunamaker. Their main stud revenue came from a horse named '*GetAWay*' and secondly from a horse named '*NharmsWay*'. Both were major stakes race winners and had proven their abilities by winning races in the Triple Crown series.

'*Sugar Creek Farms*' was owned and operated by Billy and Amanda Grayton. Their main stud revenue came from a horse named '*AtLarge*' and secondly from a horse named '*Thunderball*'. They both also were major stakes race winners and had won races in the Triple Crown series.

That's where the similarities in the two operations stopped.

Todd had interviewed with both farms before accepting the position with '*Sugar Creek Farms*'. While it was somewhat smaller and had less assets and income, Billy Grayton's honesty and ethics impressed him while Aaron Nunamaker did not make a similar impression.

According to Todd, the year he had spent working for '*Sugar Creek Farms*' had reinforced his decision to accept Billy Graytons's offer, plus he felt something was not right over at '*Nunamaker Stables*'. Aaron was a heavy gambler, and not only with his own horses, but also with most everything else. Rumors around the barns were that some significant underworld figures were now controlling '*Nunamaker Stables*', and Aaron was getting deeper and deeper into their clutches.

However, Todd's request to speak with us was about something else. It was about his concern over stud services being sold by '*Nunamaker Stables*'. He believed the horse '*GetAWay*' to be impotent, and unable to stud; however, that didn't stop the services from being sold. He believed some other horses, not '*GetAWay*', were delivering these certified services.

Todd had no proof, just some stable talk, and a conversation with a veterinarian that drank too much - but a person he trusted.

Stud service revenues from the '*Nunamaker Stables*' were significant and they were eating away at the dwindling services sold by '*Sugar Creek Farms*'. Consequently, Billy Grayton was having difficulty keeping his operations running. '*Largo*' was the horse and hope that '*Sugar Creek Farms*' future depended upon.

I interrupted his story. "Todd, this is all interesting, but it sounds like a dose of 'sour grapes' to me."

"Carson, I know, but there is more," Todd continued.

A couple of months ago, some shady characters wanting to buy '*Sugar Creek Farms*' had approached Billy Grayton, but he refused their offer and threw them out.

Todd had thought no more about his 'stable' conversations regarding '*GetAWay*' being impotent, until he was also approached by one of the characters that had tried to buy Billy out. They politely told him that any future conversation and rumors regarding '*Nunamaker Stables*' would be taken seriously, and require a follow-up visit. He knew exactly what that meant.

Todd tried to forget the conversation, the circumstances and the whole thing - until an incident last week. A part-time jockey was killed in a hit and run accident while riding one of the horses down a farm road. This jockey was also a stable worker, and the one that he had been talking to about '*Nunamaker Stables*'. The driver had killed both the jockey and the horse but never stopped.

Jack interjected. "Todd, I agree with Carson, it sounds like 'sour grapes'. If you have concerns of something illegal, or if you have suspicions about the 'hit and run', then you need to share those with the police, they are the ones who need to handle that. I'm not sure what you want Carson and me to do."

"Jack, my background isn't the cleanest it could be, and you know that. I'm thankful to have my job with '*Sugar Creek Farms*'. If I go to the authorities, they will just laugh at me, not to mention what those other characters might do! I also could lose my job, which I don't want to happen," Todd pleaded.

"Todd, let Jack and me talk about your situation over the weekend," I offered. "Leave a number where you can be reached next week, and we promise to get back to you. Is that okay?"

"Yes," he agreed. "And if you can help, I know Billy Grayton would be happy to cover your fees."

"You've already discussed this with him?" I asked with surprise.

"Not really," Todd backed off. "But I know him and he's as concerned as I am. There is something bad going on over at '*Nunamaker Stables*'." He was shaking his head as he spoke.

"Todd, does Billy Grayton know about the trouble you were in? The trouble at '*Webster Stables*'?" Jack asked.

"Yes sir. I told him all about that before he hired me. He understood; Billy is a good man," Todd replied confidently.

We talked for a few more minutes, and Todd handed us his card with a phone number where he could be reached at the farm. Then he said good-by and headed home, presumably.

"Carson, what are your thoughts?" Jack asked after Todd left.

"Jack," I answered shaking my head. "I know nothing about horses, racing and ESPECIALLY stud fees! And having the underworld involved does not surprise me one little bit, and it shouldn't surprise you either. They have their teeth in everything - the track we were at today, the hotel where we are staying and the casino where the girls are losing our money. That is not a crime I can fight or one I need to be involved in. Todd seems like a nice guy, but I have no idea what I can do to help him. Do you?"

"Nope, none, I'm sorry I got him involved in our fun. I'll call him when we get back to Memphis and tell him we can't help," Jack said finishing his drink.

"Good," I said as I stood up. "Let's go find the blackjack table. I've still got some money I haven't been able to lose today!"

As expected, the girls had given all our race winnings to the casino. However, our luck with the ponies continued to be good the next day at the track, mainly because of Liz's strange betting formula.

We returned to Memphis on Sunday evening – refreshed, revived and relieved of most of our money. Fun was had by all!

New Client

y office address is officially listed as 149 Union Avenue – L6, which means I occupy office 6, located just off the lobby of The Peabody Hotel – Memphis, Tennessee. I actually would consider my address to be 3rd Avenue – not Union, but the address has its perks.

The location itself is also handy. All my phone calls come through the hotel operator, which is also my answering service. I eat lunch and breakfast in the employee dining room at a great price. I have a beautiful lobby to greet potential clients - and please don't forget the duck show, it happens twice a day. Aside from the perverts who hang out in the lobby restrooms, I can't find a lot of fault with my office arrangements.

Besides, this is the 1960's and people are accustomed to the modern ways of doing business. Appearance is everything, or at least a close second to whatever is first. The new real estate buzz is 'location, location, location' – I think I have one of the best.

The hotel directory and telephone yellow pages show L6 occupied by 'The Drake Detective Agency'. That can be confusing, because the name on my office door reads:

Carson Reno – Private and Confidential Investigations

I am Carson Reno and always have been. There has never been a Drake working from this office, or any other in Memphis, that I am aware of. However, when I opened the agency I just could not find any rhyme or rhythm in 'The Reno Detective Agency'. Besides, everybody who has watched Perry Mason knows Paul Drake, and who knows, people may think this is a branch office or something! A little free publicity and promotion never hurt any business, just as long as they call or show-up with money.

A large number of my clients consist of damaged spouses looking for dirt and evidence on the unfaithful partner. It is possible that infidelity has made me what I am today – not a rich man, but I can pay my bills. Occasionally, I get some insurance investigation work, searching for someone who has successfully snookered the insurance company for their own goodwill, or some poor schmuck who filed false claims and skipped. But, I mostly deal with the underbelly of our society, where you find some very bad people and never make friends with anyone.

When I'm not specifically working on a case, I try to spend as much time as possible in or near the office. Another advantage of the Peabody is having access to restaurants, bars, shops and the downtown activity. So staying close is never a problem.

Afternoons and early evenings will usually find me at the Starlight Lounge, just off Winchester. Not only is it a good place to 'hang-out', it is a great place to look for clients or, in fact, look for those my clients have hired me to find! The Starlight has live entertainment starting at noon daily – yes I said noon. Everyday it is loaded with housewives who use the early part of the afternoon and evening to visit The Starlight for some drink and dance before the husband comes home from work. They cook dinner early, put it in the oven and dance on over to the Starlight for an afternoon of wine and martinis. I have a friend who calls the place "Club Menopause", and I would agree, that is an appropriate name!

Of course with the ladies come the men, generally just in search of some companionship, but sometimes in search for much more. Regardless, these are my clients, or potential clients, and I see no harm in getting to know as many of them as possible.

Rita is the head hostess at the Starlight and works some unbelievable hours. In fact, I don't remember a time when she wasn't the first to greet me regardless of the time. She was once crowned Miss Memphis and, as I understand, had a brief acting career. This lady hasn't lost a thing with age, she still has those terrific looks and manner that won her so many awards and titles. No question, she is one knockout and a classy lady who knows her stuff and knows her customers. Rita always makes sure I get an opportunity to 'meet and greet' those who are in 'distress' and might need my services. She's so good at it that I should put her on the payroll – assuming I had a payroll! However, I do make sure she gets tipped properly, whenever I get the opportunity.

My other hangout is home, or close to it. Home is a 12th floor, one bedroom apartment at the 750 Adams Complex on Manassas. A great place to call home - they have a small grocery/deli on the ground floor and a little bar in the basement called 'The Down Under'. Regardless of your condition, it is always just a short elevator ride home – and sometimes that makes good sense. Every weekend they offer live entertainment to a usually packed house. Being small, space is always limited - but my friend 'Andy', the bartender, can always seem to find me room.

~

Marcie waved at me when I entered the lobby. She had taken a message from Bert Sappington, my favorite insurance investigator. He was in his office and wanted me to call him back.

Mason 'Booker-T' Brown is the headman around the Peabody, and nobody questions that. The labor union just describes him as 'Head Porter', but Mason takes care of everything. In addition to being totally responsible for the ducks, he makes and coordinates all work schedules for the doormen, elevator operators, porters and parking garage workers. If you aren't a maid or a cook, you best look to Mason for instructions – he is the man.

Mason was dressed in his gray uniform with red leg strips, white shirt, and black tie and was cleaning around the duck fountain when I walked in. I stopped to chat.

"Mason, did the old drake that flew away ever come back?" I asked.

"No sir, Mr. Reno, but we have sure got a surprise for those folks back at the duck farm next time," Mason chuckled.

"What do you mean? You haven't lost another one have you?"

'Just the opposite. That hen, Miss Lucy, has been setting on her eggs for the past two weeks. I couldn't get her to come out of the cage, and she bit me when I tried to move her!"

"You don't mean..." I smiled.

"Yes sir, Mr. Reno – I do mean! Miss Lucy hatched out six little fellows this morning, or sometime last night. Cutest things you have ever seen, all yellow and furry. They are upstairs with her now, swimming around in the cage pond."

"Are you going to bring them down to the lobby?"

"Absolutely, we'll have a big show tomorrow morning. These five old big ducks and then Miss Lucy leading her parade with those little ones. We're going to have the newspaper come over and take some pictures. Mr. Reno, you have to come in early tomorrow and join the excitement."

"I'll try Mason. I'll try," I said walking away.

Early wasn't a word that I could even spell! Early to me would be 10 or maybe 10:30, but Mason brought those ducks down at 9 every morning and took them back upstairs at 5 every afternoon. I definitely wouldn't make the early show, but I would try for the afternoon performance.

~

Bert Sappington represented Black Diamond Insurance and I had successfully handled several cases for them. They paid a 10% recovery fee plus all expenses, whether a recovery was made or not. It was good work when I could get it.

My call to Bert was quickly answered, and he said he would meet me in my office in 10 minutes. Black Diamond's corporate office was located on Front Street and just a couple of blocks away.

Joe was in his closet office just behind mine, which was also just behind the reception desk, and Marcie's work station. He liked that! I wasn't crazy about it, but so far it hadn't been a problem.

I asked Joe to join me in my office, and we had just gotten coffee delivered when Bert walked in.

"Bert, let me introduce you to my new associate, Joe Richardson. Joe is working with me now, so you can speak freely about your case."

They shook hands, and Joe's charm quickly put Bert at ease. "Nice to meet you, Joe. I've been telling Carson for years that he needed help. I don't know about everybody else, but I'm certainly glad to see that he finally did something about it! Welcome from Black Diamond, and if you're OK in Carson's book, you are OK in mine."

"Tell us Bert, what brings you to the Drake Detective Agency?" I asked while pouring everyone coffee.

"The usual," he said. "We've got a sizable claim that seems to have some wrinkles in it. Black Diamond has made a partial settlement, but they want these wrinkles ironed out before writing that last check."

"How big of a claim and how large are the wrinkles?" I asked giving a wink toward Joe.

"Let me tell you the story, and then we can take it from there."

Bert put down his coffee cup and started his story.

The claim was for $750,000. The client had an insurance policy on his wife's jewelry – a lot of very nice and expensive jewelry. The wife had died several years ago, but his client continued the policy, saying he intended to keep the jewelry for her memory. To Bert's knowledge, there were no children or any obvious inheritance situations. So, keeping the jewelry was strange, but as long as he paid the premiums, the policy remained in effect.

The client kept the jewelry in a home safe, which had been verified by another agent. In fact, since it was stored and not worn or displayed, he actually got a break on his premiums!

About a month ago the client reported a break-in robbery, and supposedly the thief made off with all the jewelry. The police had investigated. They found evidence of a forced entry and some tampering with the safe, but bottom line, they have no suspects and the client is seeking payment on his policy.

"So what are the wrinkles?" I asked when Bert finished.

"The client is a 55 year old widower. He has no visible means of support, other than a family inheritance that originated on his wife's side of the family. Keeping the jewelry was odd, but not out of reason; however, his activities as a widower don't exactly paint a

34

picture of someone hanging onto memories, if you know what I mean," Bert chuckled.

"I do. Have you been able to check on his finances?" I asked. "Is he in need of money?"

"We've not been able to dig as deep as we would like to go, but on the surface everything seems legit. If he is strangled for money, we aren't able to determine it."

"And of course, we have the usual problems of 'where did the jewelry go' – right?" I added.

"Right," Bert confirmed. "We've done the routine searches of pawn shops, petty jewelry stores etc. If the merchandise is on the street, we can't find it."

"Bert," I asked. "Do you have an estimate of the real worth of the jewelry? I mean if he were to legitimately sell it, how much could he get?"

"That's another strange wrinkle. According the jeweler who last did an appraisal for us, these jewels would be worth twice their insured value! If he wanted the money, why not just sell them?" Bert exclaimed, throwing up both hands!

"Interesting," I said thinking. "Okay, I assume you have a file for us with all the names, dates, places and descriptions. Leave it here, and we'll get to work for Black Diamond Insurance. I assume the same arrangement, 10% recovery and full expenses regardless?"

"Yes, Carson, our usual arrangement," he nodded. "I would appreciate weekly updates and immediate notification if/when you come up with anything."

"Done," I said to Bert. "Either Joe or I will be in touch."

Bert handed me a small file, then we shook hands and he left.

I opened the file; Joe and I reviewed it together.

The client's name was Elliot Farnsworth, and he had a Germantown, Tennessee address. In addition to an address, phone and personal information on Farnsworth, the file contained a detailed description on the jewelry, all 17 pieces, plus a photograph of each. It also contained a collective photo showing each piece that was insured by Black Diamond Insurance.

This was all we needed.

I handed the file to Joe. "Okay, Mr. Private Detective, here is your first case," I joked.

"Terrific! What should I do? Where do I start?" he was excited.

"Start with the police – Shelby County Chief of Detectives Larry Parker, in particular. Larry will point you in the right direction. Find out all you can about the reported robbery, the times, details etc. Larry will see that the files are made available to you. Then latch onto this guy. Follow him and make notes of his habits, his travels, and his friends. Let's see what makes Elliot Farnsworth tick. If he has the jewelry, he might try to sell it and not pawn it. He knows what it's worth, and knows it would take someone with a big wallet to buy it, not just any broker."

"Okay. Any other ideas?" Joe was taking notes as we talked.

"A couple," I added. "If he has the jewelry, and doesn't plan on selling it, then he must have other plans. They could be anything from a girlfriend, to trading the things for some woman's favors. Make yourself very familiar with every piece of jewelry in that file, familiar enough that you would recognize any piece if you saw it somewhere it didn't belong. Stay with this guy, and if he's dirty, it won't take long to find out."

"Will do, I'm headed over to the police station now. Anything else?" He was almost too excited to talk!

"Yes. Report to me daily, no exceptions. And keep up with your expenses in detail. Okay?"

"Done," he said as he rushed out the door. I was hoping he didn't trip over somebody trying to get out of the lobby!

I had just started on the mail when the phone rang, it was Marcie and she had Jack Logan on the line. I told her to put him through.

"Hey buddy," I said laughing. "You still counting your winnings from the horse races?"

"Hell, Carson, what winnings? Everything we won at the races, we lost at the casino. I just wish Liz had a system for blackjack like she has with the ponies, we would be rich men!"

"Me too. What's up? You want to have lunch?" I asked.

"Yes, that is exactly why I called. I need to talk with you. When can you make it?" Jack quizzed.

"I'm leaving as we speak," I replied. "See you at the Rendezvous."

I was already halfway through my first beer, when Jack finally came down the stairs and joined me at my table. We both ordered our usual lunch rib plate, and I could sense Jack had something important to talk about.

"You seem on edge," I said. "What's up?"

"I am. You want to guess who called and hired me this morning?" Jack asked, sipping his beer.

"Nope, no idea. Just tell me and we'll skip the foreplay," I shot back.

"Todd Randal, he's in jail in Humboldt – charged with murder!"

"WHAT?" I shouted, as I almost turned over my beer!

"He's charged with the murder of Aaron Nunamaker. Do you remember that name?" Jack asked with a smile.

"I sure do," I answered quickly. "You have any details?"

"Let me tell what I know from my conversation with Todd and with the sheriff, Leroy Epsee. Sometime Saturday night Nunamaker's barn burned, along with most of his horses, including his prize-breeding thoroughbreds. Among the ashes they found Aaron Nunamaker, burned beyond recognition. They only identified him by some jewelry he was always known to wear; however, he didn't burn to death. He had a bullet through the heart, and most likely from a high powered rifle. Also, among the ashes they found a rifle - a 30/30 with Todd's initials engraved on the receiver. Matching tire prints also puts Todd's truck at the barn and they were made sometime before or during the fire. Evidently, it had rained Saturday morning, so the timing of the tracks was easily determined. And if the tracks weren't enough, Todd was also witnessed at the barn late Saturday evening. He was seen by one of Nunamaker's jockey's, an Eddie Merrick. So, Leroy arrested Todd late yesterday, and Todd called me first thing this morning."

"And what is Todd's story?" I was interested.

"He admits to being at the barn. He even admits to an argument with Nunamaker, but he says he didn't kill him. He says Aaron Nunamaker was alive and yelling his lungs out when he left."

"What did they argue about? Did Todd say?" I asked.

"The things he discussed with you and me on Friday night in Hot Springs. He claims that after he left our hotel, he drove back to Humboldt, arriving late Friday night/early Saturday morning back at '*Sugar Creek Farms*'. Todd says he slept in Saturday morning, and then decided to drive over and confront Nunamaker that evening. He said he told Nunamaker that he knew about the false stud fee certification and that he intended to let everyone know. He said he also told him he knew about his Mafia connections and would tell everyone about that too! He claims they argued, had loud words and even almost came to blows, but Todd said when he left the barn, Nunamaker was alive. Mad as hell, but alive."

I leaned back, thought for a minute then asked, "What do you want to do?"

"I've got court tomorrow and can't leave until after that. There's no bail for Todd, but evidently, Billy Grayton has agreed to handle all fees associated with his defense. I need you, if you can, to get yourself to Humboldt and start digging. See what you can find before I have to make a plea for Todd," Jack requested.

"What is your gut feeling?" I asked Jack seriously. "You think he did it?"

"I honestly don't know. If he isn't guilty, he sure as hell looks guilty. However, I am a pretty good reader of the truth when somebody tells me something. I think he is telling me the truth, or at least PART of the truth. My mind tells me one thing and my instinct another. Guess we'll just have to sort through the puzzle and see where everything fits," Jack suggested.

"Interesting," I said to myself.

"Can you possibly make it to Humboldt tonight?" Jack requested. "I would like all the information I can get before I meet with Todd. He's lying about something, I just don't know what."

"Yep, can do," I answered. "I've got an insurance case with Black Diamond, but Joe is going to chase that down. I can manage him from Humboldt, I think. I'll get my stuff together and leave this afternoon. When will you be there?"

"Tomorrow late, or Wednesday latest," Jack said thinking. "Meanwhile, we'll stay in touch and I'll let Todd know you will be seeing him sometime tomorrow."

We hurriedly finished lunch, and I rushed back to the office and went through the mail. There was nothing important, so I told Marcie I was headed to Humboldt, and she would be able to reach me at Chiefs. I also asked her to brief Joe when he came back to the office, and tell him I would phone him this evening or tomorrow. Then, I made a quick stop by my apartment for some clean laundry; the long weekend had put me behind, and I had no idea how long I would be in Humboldt.

On my way out of town, I drove by Liz's apartment and left her a note on the door. She was out of town and not expected back until the end of the week, but I felt better letting her know I would be gone for a few days.

Then I rolled down the windows on the old Ford, tuned the radio to some jazz music and pointed it toward Humboldt. It knew the way!

I still drive a 56 Ford, left over from college. It's black, 4 doors, V8, manual transmission and nothing fancy. It is however, very functional and very dependable – not to mention it is built like a tank. It is also very fast – fast enough to get you into trouble quickly and, hopefully, fast enough to get you out of trouble just as quick.

Humboldt

*I*t was almost dark when I pulled into Chief's parking lot. As usual, they were crowded and I had difficulty finding the Ford a good spot to rest. An endless line of cars circled the building – occasionally stopping for curb service, but mostly just participating in the nightly ritual – which would continue until the wee hours of the morning.

Chiefs Restaurant and Bar

Chiefs is a popular local hangout located on North 22nd. Avenue in Humboldt. It is owned and operated by a couple of close friends, Ronnie and Nickie Woodson. Given the opportunity, you would find it an unusual and terrific place to stay and visit. They offer an indoor restaurant and bar, outside curb service and small cottage rooms for traveling guests. You can't miss it – it's located right under the big neon Indian Chief sign!

41

Chiefs Cottages

Nickie and husband Ronnie have owned and operated Chiefs for as long as I could remember. He runs the kitchen and does most of the cooking. Nickie handles everything else – including Cottage rentals, the books, the inventory and keeping Ronnie in line. Ronnie has a 'wandering eye' - and probably other 'wandering' parts – which keeps Nickie busy. However, along with a couple of waitresses and Nickie's supervision, everything always seemed to go like clockwork. She also manages the carhops who serve outside patrons.

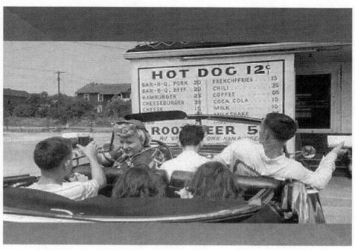

Carhops are a different breed – they are either good or just plain terrible. Tommy is my favorite and has been with Nickie and Ronnie since the beginning. I guess you would call him the 'team leader' carhop. Whatever you need – and I mean 'whatever you need' - Tommy Trubush is your man. Everybody knows there is a lot of underage drinking – but Tommy keeps it straight and never lets it get out of hand. I have many times seen him put tough guys on the ground, and when he asked someone to leave – they leave. He runs the outside show – no question about it.

~

Nickie was engaged in a serious conversation with one of her customers and she didn't see me enter. I managed to find a stool at the end of the bar and ordered my usual Jack Daniels and Coke from an unknown waitress – obviously a new employee.

The cute new waitress quickly delivered my drink along with a smile and a 'thank you'. Nickie finally finished her conversation, then made her way back behind the bar, still not noticing me sitting at the end of the bar.

Nickie had her back to me when I yelled over the jukebox music, "Hey, bartender, my drink has a hair in it!"

That got her attention, and finally Nickie looked my way. "Carson Reno, welcome back to the Heartland of America! How do you always manage to slip in without me seeing you?" Nickie said laughing and walking toward me.

"It's not difficult," I joked. "I'm a detective, remember?"

"Remember? No one around here can forget! You come, and then you go, leaving dead people in your wake. Trust me, you may be gone away from Humboldt, but you are NEVER forgotten! Now, let me see about that hair in your drink." Nickie was reaching for my drink.

Before I could tell her I was kidding, she already had her hand in my glass and was moving her fingers around the bottom. "Okay, I got it," she yelled. Then she removed her hand and pretended to analyze this invisible hair. "It's not from anyone I recognize, maybe you brought it with you. You want to keep it, or should I throw it away?" she asked while showing me the 'invisible' hair.

"Nickie, you are priceless! Would you happen to have a room for a tired detective?"

"Absolutely," she replied. "Would you prefer one of our upgraded suites, or just regular deluxe accommodations?"

"Upgraded? Suites? What the hell are you talking about? I just need a room!" I answered with a frown.

"Ronnie has painted the inside of some of our cottages. That's an upgrade – right?" Nickie had a big smile.

"Yes, I guess so, but aren't we stretching it a bit? Suites?" I laughed.

She glared at me. "Tell you what Mr. Reno, you trot yourself up to the Royal Court and check out their rooms. If ours aren't 'suites' compared to what they rent, then the drinks are on me! Deal?"

"No, it is not a deal," I answered with a nod. "Just give me my usual and I'll forget that I ever brought it up. Okay?"

"You got it, your regular Cottage 4. It has fresh paint and everything. Now, would you like something to eat? I'll try to see if we can't keep stray hairs out of your food!" she laughed.

"Yes, I believe I would. Please add one of Ronnie's burgers, and while you're asking, please freshen my drink. I'll be outside on the payphone," I said as I got up and walked back out the front door.

I needed to make a call and would, of course, need to use the phone located outside. Whatever idiot installed the inside payphone next to the jukebox had to have been drunk or crazy – probably both. Nobody used that phone because nobody could HEAR while using that phone. The jukebox only stopped playing when Nickie or Ronnie turned it off, which was never. It probably has a thousand country songs already lined up for play. People just keep putting money in it and wondering why their song isn't playing next, it would take a week to cycle through and reach their selection. No matter, they still keep dropping quarters and punching buttons.

My first call was to Liz's Memphis apartment – no answer. As I figured, she had not returned from her flight, and the note I left had requested her to call me at Chiefs.

My second call was to Leroy Epsee, Sheriff of Gibson County and he wasn't in either. Leroy would need to be my first stop tomorrow.

Back inside, Nickie had me a fresh drink and one of Ronnie's terrific hamburgers. She came over to talk when I sat back down on my stool.

"Let me guess. Your being in town has something to do with that guy burning up in his barn – that Nunamaker fellow who owned a stud farm, right?" She was fishing.

"Yes, sorta. And it's a horse farm, not a stud farm! They have racehorses and also breed their championship thoroughbreds. Now, don't start asking me questions I am not supposed to answer. Okay?"

"What does Carson Reno know about stud farms? Wait - let me rephrase that. What does Carson Reno know about HORSE stud farms?" Nickie laughed.

"Very little," I happily replied. "What do you know?"

"I know there is a lot of money in that business," Nickie perked up. "If I could sell Ronnie to a stud service, I could quit this bar and go lay on a beach somewhere. Unfortunately, he just THINKS he's a stud and the proof is in the delivery. Trust me, I know."

"Ha! Ronnie might just take you up on the offer. The good news is, I know you are kidding." At least I thought she was.

"Yes, I'm just teasing you," she said. "But the local news said that they had arrested someone, are you working for him?"

"In a way, yes, I do know the man, and Jack will be representing him and I'm here helping Jack. Did you know Aaron Nunamaker?" I asked stirring my fresh drink.

"Never met him," Nickie said turning up her nose. "Carson, those people run in different circles. Chiefs was not on their top 10 list of favorite restaurants, trust me!"

"I understand. What have you heard about it?" I was curious. "Any bar talk or rumors?"

"Not really," Nickie offered. "Just that they had arrested the trainer from one of the other ranches for the murder, a Todd Randal, or something like that."

"Yep, that's the story," I was being evasive. "Listen, I'll need the room for several days, I hope that's okay. I'll let you know."

"It's yours for as long as you need it," Nickie said as she got up and walked away.

I finished the drink and burger then decided I'd had enough of that damn jukebox for one evening. I said goodnight to Nickie and then waved at the cute new waitress (she waved back!); however, I made it a short evening. I had a full day tomorrow!

Gibson County Sheriff's Office and Jail

Somehow, I managed to get an early start (10:00 AM). It was overcast, cloudy and I could smell rain in the air, as I grabbed a cup of Nickie's coffee to go and quickly headed over to the Gibson County Sheriff's office and jail.

Deputy Jeff Cole was manning the desk, and said that Leroy was on his way to the office. Leroy Epsee was the Gibson County Sheriff and an old and trusted friend. I had the greatest respect for him, and I believe he had that same respect for me.

"Jeff, do you guys still have Todd Randal upstairs?" I asked heading for the coffeepot.

"Yep. And from what Leroy tells me, he'll be staying with us until after the trial and sentencing," Jeff said frankly. "That is, of course, unless some lawyer gets a change of venue and moves the proceedings out of our county. Otherwise, he's ours to house and feed until the court tells us something different."

"Did you know Todd before his arrest?" I asked wondering.

"Nope. I don't think anybody here at the sheriff's office did," Jeff speculated. "I know Leroy didn't, and I'm pretty sure Deputy Perry didn't either. He certainly was never in any trouble around here, that I'm aware of; however, he does have a record. Did you know that?"

"Yes, I know about that. How well did you know Aaron Nunamaker?" I was changing the subject.

"I didn't really know him either, but Leroy did. He used to take his kids out to the stables for horse rides. According to what I heard Leroy say, Mr. Nunamaker was an ok guy," Jeff added.

I saw Leroy's cruiser pull up and park while Jeff and I were talking. Leroy was shaking his head when he walked in door.

"Well, well, well – Mr. Carson Reno. If I were a betting man, I could have won a lot of money on a bet that you would show up in Humboldt this week," he was still shaking his head and laughing.

"See, sometimes your bad vices can become good vices, if you take advantage of them," I nodded.

"It wouldn't have been a fair bet," Leroy said as he thumbed through his messages. "I already know Jack Logan is Todd Randal's lawyer, and you following along behind him is old news. I suppose you are here to see Mr. Randal?"

"Yes, but first I would like to talk with you. You got a few minutes?" I requested.

"Sure. You've already got coffee, so let me grab some and let's go in my office," Leroy said as he headed for the coffee maker.

He got coffee and we retreated into his office to have some privacy. Leroy asked Jeff to hold his calls, as he turned and closed the door.

"Carson, I know why you are here. So let me tell you the official version, and then you can visit with Todd. Okay?"

"Okay, sounds good," I agreed.

"We got a relayed call from the fire department at about 11PM Saturday night. They had received a call from someone on the Nunamaker property saying that a barn was on fire. At this point, we don't know who made that call; however, I doubt it was Susan Nunamaker, but I have not questioned her yet. Anyway, Scotty was on duty and took the relayed call from the fire department. He called me at home and then responded immediately to the fire. I was about 10 minutes behind him.

There wasn't much we could do when we got there, other than just sit back and watch it burn. We knew there were horses in the barn, but there was absolutely no way to get them out. The flames from the old wood and hay just made it a raging inferno. Actually, it was over rather quickly, I estimate it didn't take longer than 30 minutes for the whole place to burn completely to the ground.

Then I sent Scotty home, because it was the end of his shift, and I stayed the rest of the night. Jeff joined me at daylight and that's when we got a good look at the horror and damage. Evidently, someone had moved horses from an adjoining barn because there were horse carcasses everywhere, and more than would ever be housed in that barn. It wasn't until we began moving the rubble, that we saw a human corpse among the carnage. That's when I called the coroner, Dr. Barker.

Considering the condition of the body, I figured it would take quite some time for identification. But, Dr. Barker was able to make a quick identification using some jewelry item that Aaron Nunamaker always wore. He also was able to determine that Aaron Nunamaker had been shot, at close range, and probably with a high powered rifle!

We began to question the stable workers and this Eddie Merrick was the only one who had anything to add. He said he had left Mr.

Nunamaker working in the stable at approximately 8 or 8:30 PM. Evidently, Merrick remained on the property, because he says that he saw Todd Randal drove up at about 9 and disappear into the stable where Aaron Nunamaker was working. He claims to have heard loud voices, but couldn't tell me about anything they were saying. Eddie claims he left the property at 9:30 and Todd Randal was still there, in the stable with Aaron Nunamaker.

Among the rubble we found a rifle belonging to Todd Randal and also found fresh tire prints outside the barn. Jeff made impressions of the tire prints and brought them along when we drove out to '*Sugar Creek Farms*' that afternoon to question Todd. The tire prints matched, and based upon his statements to me, I placed him under arrest. The DA signed a warrant yesterday and Mr. Todd Randal has been officially charged with the murder of Aaron Nunamaker. I'm sure many other charges will follow."

"What was it about Todd's statement that made you arrest him?" I questioned.

"Because he first denied being anywhere near '*Nunamaker Farms*' on Saturday. Then, when I confronted him with the tire tracks and Eddie Merrick's statement, he admitted that he was there, but said he left at 10:00. He also, finally admitted to having an argument with Aaron Nunamaker. He said they were arguing over business and how '*Nunamaker Farms*' was charging for uncertified stud services. He said he told Aaron he was going to expose him to the board, and that's when Aaron Nunamaker became violent and threatened him with bodily harm, so he left. He claims he left at 10 and Aaron Nunamaker was alive – mad, but alive."

"Why don't you believe Todd's story?" I asked.

"First, because he lied, and then for all the reasons you know and understand all too well. Motive, Presence, Ability and Weapon - his rifle was found at the murder scene. We don't have confirmation that his rifle was actually the murder weapon, but hopefully we will get that information today or tomorrow.

We know he was there at a time close to when Aaron Nunamaker was shot. We know he argued with Aaron Nunamaker, and we know that his rifle was found at the scene. We also know he lied to me about even being at the farm, and we know Todd Randal has a record."

"Wait a minute, Leroy!" I protested. "He has a record, but nothing violent. His past crimes concerned document falsification about working stud horses. Basically, the same crime he was accusing Aaron Nunamaker of. That won't hold water, and you know it." I was probably pushing Leroy too hard.

"Carson, I'm sure all that will come to the surface," he shot back. "If Aaron Nunamaker was doing something illegal, that will come out during our investigation or at the trial. If Tony Randal was helping Aaron Nunamaker do something illegal, then that will come out, too."

"Oh, now I get it," I huffed. "I see where you are going with that. They were in it together and had a falling out, right?"

"Carson, let's just leave it at that. Do you want to see Todd Randal or not?" he demanded getting up from his chair.

"I do, but I have a question for you. Where was Susan Nunamaker during this whole fiasco? You said you haven't talked to her. She didn't even show up at the barn fire? Did she tell anybody her husband might have been in there? What's her story?" I guess that was more than one question, huh?

"I'm waiting to ask her. Right now, we don't know where Susan Nunamaker is," Leroy answered slowly.

"Oh shit," I said to myself.

"Don't go there, Carson," Leroy cautioned. "We'll find her and I don't suspect she's been harmed. Maybe she's just scared, but whatever Todd's motives were, he succeeded in putting 'Nunamaker Farms' out of business. With a horse farm that offers racing horses and stud horses, you need horses. They all perished in that fire, and except for a few saddle ponies that stayed in the pasture overnight and a few other workhorses in another barn, there is nothing left. This was a vicious crime, and I don't just mean the murder. Anger, greed or whatever caused Todd Randal to go far beyond just shooting the competition – he killed innocent animals and killed a healthy business. This crime has far reaching affects, and affects that go way beyond the victim and his family!"

I don't think I had ever seen Leroy this upset.

"Okay, but let's don't hang him, just yet," I suggested. "I had a chance to meet and talk with Todd Randal a few days ago before all this happened. He didn't seem like such an evil person then, but perhaps I misjudged him. Regardless, can I talk with him now?"

"Alright. Do you want to use my conference room, or would you prefer to talk in his cell?" Leroy was being tough.

"I'll choose the conference room. I've seen your jail once, and that was enough!" I answered frankly.

Leroy took me over to the conference room and then went upstairs to get Todd Randal.

Todd Randal

*T*odd Randal wasn't a large man, he was about my size, and I estimated him to be in his middle to late forties. When I first saw him working in the paddock at Oaklawn, he was easy to spot among the trainers and horse handlers. Unlike the others, he wasn't wearing the traditional riding suit, boots, hat etc. He was dressed for business, not show. Tan pants, blue work shirt and boots that were suited for work, not riding. He was also wearing a simple vest, showing the racing colors of '*Sugar Creek Farms*', along with an armband that denoted his status as a trainer.

He also wore a hat, like most of the other people in the paddock. But like his clothes, his hat was more suited for his job as trainer and not for show. The hat wasn't cloth or felt and didn't have a fancy bill or tassel; it was a narrow brim semi-straw hat. A hat that I'm sure he wore most every day while working and training his horses.

What I saw in Todd Randal at the paddock was a man truly focused on his work. He was there to put his best horse in the field, and he was not there to impress the crowd.

When I saw Todd later at the Arlington, he appeared exactly the same. Minus the vest and armband, he was the same person I had watched go about his duties in the paddock; focused, dedicated and a real believer in his skills and accomplishments.

The man that Leroy brought downstairs and sat across the conference room table seemed – different. Gone was the confidence and focus and replaced by a county issued orange jumpsuit and handcuffs - both compliments of the Gibson County Sheriff's Department.

But the real difference was the absence of his hat. Todd Randal was almost bald; something the hat had hidden very well. Without the hat, he seemed to have aged 10 years from our last meeting at the Arlington.

Todd entered and took his seat in silence. He shook his head to refuse the coffee and cigarette offerings from Leroy.

"Would you like to be alone?" Leroy asked me directly.

"Yes, for a few minutes, if you don't mind. Are the handcuffs necessary?" I asked Leroy with a frown.

"Yes they are. I'll be in my office," Leroy responded as he left.

I spent the first few minutes, pacing back and forth in front of the table, trying to decide how I wanted to start this conversation.

"Todd, I'm going to skip the usual question and answer shit," I started. "I've heard Leroy's story, I've heard what you told Leroy and I've heard what you told Jack. And I'm pretty sure I'll get to hear them again. But, I need you to answer one question for me. What was going through your mind when you decided to drive over and confront Aaron Nunamaker? Did you really expect to resolve anything?"

I don't think Todd had looked directly at me since he had entered the room. Showing embarrassment, he mostly stared at the floor. Hearing my question, he finally looked at me for a moment and then back at the floor. It was several seconds before he spoke. "Carson, I don't know. Reflecting back, I guess I can only say that I was mad. Unless you've been around these animals and this business, it can be difficult to understand. There is a sort of respect that you develop for the horses, the business and the work. We assume that everyone who works in the business has that same respect, but Aaron Nunamaker didn't have that respect. I felt I needed to do something about it," he answered frankly.

"Well, it seems you did! They've got little more than ashes to put in his coffin. Did that make you feel better?" I was talking straight at him, and he continued to stare at the floor.

"Carson, I didn't kill him," he pleaded. "He was alive when I left that barn. He was mad and he was yelling, but he was alive. I swear!"

I was still pacing in front of the table as I spoke. "Save that for the jury, I think you're going to need it. Can you explain how your rifle ended up in that barn?"

Todd finally looked up and glared at me. "No, I can't," he answered shaking his head. "The rifle stays behind the seat of my truck, and I honestly don't remember the last time I took it out or even the last time I saw it. Someone could have taken that rifle most any time, and I would never have known it. My truck is never locked anyway; nobody locks their vehicles around here, no reason to."

"Okay, Todd. I've got one more question and then I'm leaving. If you didn't kill Aaron Nunamaker, then who do you think did?" I asked.

"I don't know," he said still looking at me. "But there is someone you need to talk to, they may have some ideas."

"Who?" I almost shouted.

"Doctor Jack Preston. He's a veterinarian. His office is about two miles out the Trenton highway. If he's sober, he'll be there. If he's not, then he could be anywhere."

"Is this the veterinarian you mentioned to Jack and me at the Arlington?" I was trying to remember.

"Yes," he said. "Find him and he can tell you a lot about Mr. Aaron Nunamaker and '*Nunamaker Stables*', I promise."

"Okay, I'll do that." I opened the door, then turned around to ask him one last question. "Todd, you spoke about respect, and how Aaron Nunamaker didn't have that respect for the animals or the business. Did you have that respect when you were arrested for your activities at '*Webster Stables*'?"

"No – I didn't, but I learned," he answered with an honest voice. "That made me a better horseman, a better trainer and a better man. I got a second chance, and now I sit here and hope I get a third!"

"Well. I can only promise that Jack and I will do what we can. Just don't lie to us," I ordered.

"I won't," he said nodding. Unfortunately, that was a lie too!

I closed the conference room door and left Todd sitting and staring at the floor.

Leroy was not in his office, but Jeff was still at the front desk.

"Jeff," I asked, "has Jack Logan checked in with Todd this morning?"

Jeff looked up from his paperwork, "No sir, at least I wasn't here if he called. You need me to give him a message if he does?" he asked.

"No, it's not necessary. I'll catch up with him later," I mumbled as I walked out the door and got back in the Ford.

~

My destination was '*Sugar Creek Farms*' and a visit with my friend, Billy Grayton. Since it was in the general direction I would be headed, I decided to drive by the office of Doctor Jack Preston and see if he was sober and in his office today.

Dr. Jack Preston's Office

It was not my lucky day.

No vehicles were present and no one answered my knock. Hanging on the door was one of those clock signs that read "BE BACK IN.......". Unfortunately, the hands had been removed from the clock; likely by some angry customer tired of waiting on Dr. Preston to sober up!

56

But, taped to the inside of the glass was a faded photograph of Dr. Preston. Probably used for an advertising or publicity flyer. Well, at least I knew what he looks like!

Dr. Jack Preston – Veterinarian

'Sugar Creek Farms' is located on Esquire Hunt Road, which runs parallel and west of Highway 45; it was a beautiful area. From Humboldt, the drive is a short distance out the Gibson Wells Highway, then taking Esquire Hunt Road north. However, since I was leaving from Dr. Preston's unoccupied office, my route is Hwy 45 north to Fruitland and then west to Esquire Hunt Road.

About a mile up the highway, I noticed in my rear view mirror a two door 1959 black Chevrolet Impala following about a quarter mile back. I thought I had seen the car previously, before stopping at Dr. Preston's office and after leaving the sheriff's office. There were two men in the car.

The car followed when I turned at Fruitland and kept its quarter mile distance until I made the turn into '*Sugar Creek Farms*'. It didn't turn, but as it drove by I noticed Shelby County tags. I would need to check that out later.

Sugar Creek Farms

Amanda Grayton greeted me at the door. Billy was down at one of the stables and she sent word with a stable worker for him to come back to the house and join us.

I really didn't know Amanda Grayton. Billy had met her while he was at college, and other than at a few social functions, we had not talked much. She was quite attractive, short in height and had auburn hair trimmed almost like a man's. Today and always, she dressed the part of a wealthy rancher, never jeans or any clothes that would offer a hint of work, but expensive western outfits with very expensive leather boots.

Billy was just the opposite. I rarely ever remember seeing him in anything other than jeans and a pearl button cowboy shirt. Even his formal attire would include a string tie – he was the horseman.

'*Sugar Creek Farms*' was the product of Billy's grandfather, and Billy's father had carried on its rich tradition. Billy's mother and father had both passed away within a year of his college graduation. After Billy finished school, he came back to '*Sugar Creek Farms*' to follow what his grandfather and father had started. At some point, Amanda joined him at '*Sugar Creek Farms*' and they have been fixtures in Gibson County and the Horse Community of West Tennessee ever since.

Amanda escorted me through their spacious home and onto the open patio, which joined their den area. One of the servants brought Amanda and me ice tea, and we chatted while waiting for Billy to join us.

"Amanda, I'm sorry I've never visited your home before. This is absolutely lovely. I know you and Billy are proud." I said sincerely.

"Yes Carson, we are," she said while showing her lovely smile. "And we have some pretty good race horses too, in case you didn't know."

"Oh, but I do know! I was at Oaklawn a few days ago and picked up a nice winning ticket with your horse '*Largo*'."

"Really? I guess that is where you met Todd Randal," she speculated. "Billy told me that you and Jack Logan will be working to get him out of this awful mess. It is just terrible what happened to Aaron Nunamaker, but I know Todd had nothing to do with it. Todd has been a blessing to '*Sugar Creek Farms*'. His training of '*Largo*', and all our horses, has made the best out of what has not been the greatest of times."

"What do you mean?" I think I knew what she meant, but I wanted to hear it from her.

Before she could answer, Billy pulled up on his tractor.

"Carson Reno, why does it take trouble to make you come see me?" Billy joked as he got off the tractor and we shook hands.

"My apology Billy, I know it has been too long. Work, work and then more work always seems to get in the way."

"That may be true, but in addition to your parents still living in Humboldt, I happen to know you have been spending quite a bit of time here on other matters. So, skip the bullshit and I'll accept your apology! Let's have some iced tea and talk about Todd," he said.

We visited for a while, and he really didn't share anything with me that I hadn't learned already. Todd lived in a house located on the farm and had been a model employee, plus a real asset to '*Sugar Creek Farms*'. Billy had nothing to add about Todd's coming and going on Saturday, but was absolutely certain that he could not have killed Aaron Nunamaker. Then, he said something that convinced me Todd Randal was an innocent man.

"Carson, I'm a good judge of people," he offered. "But, given the right circumstances, even good people can do bad things. Todd Randal might have been capable of killing Aaron Nunamaker; I don't know the circumstances, but he was not capable of killing those horses, and you can take that to the bank! And whoever killed Aaron, killed those horses – that would not have been Todd Randal!" Billy was dead serious as he spoke.

"Okay, Billy, suppose I buy that. What is your opinion about the trouble Todd was in at '*Webster Stables*' before he came to work for you?"

"What trouble?" he asked shaking his head.

"You mean Todd didn't tell you about the false stud certification problems he had at '*Webster Stables*'? He didn't tell you that Jack had defended him and, basically, kept him from going to jail?"

"Nope, first I have heard about it." Billy said frankly.

"Well that's odd, because Todd told Jack and I that he had told you all about it and you understood. Why would he lie?" I questioned.

"I don't know. Why don't you tell me about it now?" Billy requested.

I told Billy the story, as I knew it. And then suggested that the next time he talked with Todd, to get more details.

When I finished, Billy looked at me with absolutely no expression and said, "Okay, but that doesn't change my opinion of Todd one bit. It might have given me second thoughts about hiring him, but now that he has worked for me a year, it makes no difference. Todd has had a significant and positive impact on '*Sugar Creek Farms*'. Without him, I don't think we would have made it this far. Regardless of what he has done in the past, I am only measuring him by what I have seen him do. My statement still stands, he could not have killed Aaron, because he could not have killed those horses."

"Okay, Billy. You brought it up, tell me about your problems. What has been going on?" I asked.

Billy looked me in the eye as he answered. "We have two of the finest stud horses in West Tennessee – '*AtLarge*' and '*Thunderball*'. Their credentials are indisputable, but I have to beg owners to bring their qualified mares. My stud business is off 75% and '*Nunamaker Stables*' business is up 75%. We've been hanging our hopes and last dollars on '*Largo*', thinking that perhaps we needed something new to offer. Of course, now there is 'no' '*Nunamaker Stables*', so maybe things can start heading in the right direction again. Listen Carson, I'm sorry for what happened over there, but I'm not sorry for the benefits it brings '*Sugar Creek Farms*'. I hate to say that, but it is the way I feel."

"Billy, I understand, but that's one of the reasons the sheriff is convinced Todd is guilty – he did it to save '*Sugar Creek Farms*'."

"Well, whoever did it did just that," Billy nodded. "They saved '*Sugar Creek Farms*', but it wasn't Todd, trust me."

Billy poured us another glass of tea and I asked, "Do you have any ideas or suggestions about where I might start to look for the killer?"

"Yes, start with that drunken veterinarian, Dr. Preston. Then, you need to talk with the Nunamaker jockey, Eddie Merrick; I don't trust that guy. For some background, you should also talk with my number one jockey, Miguel Rivera. He might be able to point you in some different directions."

"Okay, I'll do that. One last question, and then I'll leave you alone. Todd told Jack and me that some mob type people came to see you about buying '*Sugar Creek Farms*'. Do you know if they had any connections to Aaron Nunamaker?" I asked.

"They came to see me and I threw them out. Regarding the mob connection to Aaron Nunamaker, it was rumored, but I have no first hand knowledge, nor do I put much faith in rumors. So, the answer is, I don't know." As before, Billy was 'matter of fact' with his response.

We visited for another half-hour and then I pointed the Ford toward Humboldt. I did not see the 59 Impala on my trip back.

~

When I finally parked the Ford in front of my cottage, it was already after 5 and happy hour at Chiefs.

I had barely gotten settled on a barstool when Nickie showed up with my Jack/Coke. "Hey handsome, you been fighting crime today?"

"Absolutely, and with both hands! The streets are safe tonight," I joked. "However, it looks like you might have most of the county population in here. Any special occasion or is this just a normal Tuesday afternoon drinking crowd?"

"Normal crowd, and thank goodness for the bar business, it seems like nobody eats out anymore," Nickie said with disgust.

"Nickie, speaking of your bar business, who is the new waitress, bartender or whatever she is?" I asked, as I pointed my glass in the direction of the young girl who had served me yesterday.

"You like that huh?" Nickie said grinning. "Her name is Barbie. You know, like the doll? Want me to fix you up? She's available."

"No, I don't want you to fix me up!" I protested. "But she does seem popular with the crowd. They are actually paying more attention to her than the jukebox – and that's saying something!"

"She has definitely been good for business. I've got new regulars who just come in to drink and look at her ass! But we're here to please the customer with whatever they want," she giggled.

"Not meaning to touch on a sore subject," I said reluctantly. "But doesn't that cause you some problems with Ronnie? I mean, I know he has a tendency to ah…wander…if that's a good way to put it."

"That is a good way to put it, all right. Except he doesn't wander – he gets LOST! However, Barbie does offer some benefits."

"Oh, yeah, like what?" I asked with a grin.

"Well, she keeps Ronnie in heat all day and I always know where to find him. And, on occasion, I can take advantage of that heat when we get home at night! Know what I mean?" she laughed.

"Nickie, I love it when you talk dirty. Do I have any messages?"

"I was not talking dirty and YES you have messages. You always have messages – I spend all day taking your messages – nothing new there. Let me find my order pad and I'll get them for you."

Nickie was the only one who could actually HEAR anything on the pay phone over the jukebox. I never understood how she did that, but she would take my messages on her little green waitress pad, just like taking a hamburger order.

"Okay, Mr. Reno, here are your messages. Jack Logan called and said he was still tied up in court, but would be here tomorrow and plan on dinner. Joe Richardson called and said he was suspicious of the police burglary report, but had more checking to do. He also said you could call him at his apartment tonight, if you needed to talk. Marcie called to tell you there were 6 new baby ducks in the fountain, and that you didn't have any new client calls. And Elizabeth Teague called and wanted to know why you were in Humboldt."

"Where was Elizabeth Teague calling from?" I asked looking up.

"Mr. Reno, I have no idea where she was calling from," she snapped. "I don't provide information or ask questions, I just take messages. If you can't control your women, don't expect help from here. And who is this Joe Richardson? Your new partner?"

"He isn't a partner, he is an associate and he works for me. Hopefully, you will get to meet him soon; you'll like him. He is a nice guy and a big help to me."

"I'm looking forward to it," she said. "Now, you better get your little butt outside on the phone, and report in with Elizabeth Teague before you get in more trouble. I'll refresh your drink while you cry in the phone!"

"I love you, Nickie," I laughed. "I'll be back in a minute."

My first call was to Liz, but got no answer at her Memphis or Humboldt number. She could be anywhere, and she would call back. I decided to not call Joe yet, let him use his head. As long as he followed my instructions and checked in everyday, I was fine. Maybe I should get him up here to help with Todd Randal, after I gathered more detail.

I called for Leroy and, of course, he wasn't in. Scotty was at the desk, and I asked him to tell Leroy that I planned to visit '*Nunamaker Stables*' tomorrow and would like him to join me, if he could. I also told him that Jack Logan was delayed, but would be in town tomorrow. He should let Todd know, if he didn't know already.

Back on my barstool, I ordered one of Ronnie's steaks and finished the evening making small talk with Nickie. And, along with the rest of the male customers, I watched the new little waitress wiggle her wares around Chiefs. She was definitely nice to look at.

Nunamaker Stables

$\mathcal{A}$s the skies had promised, it was misting rain when I woke. I ate Ronnie's breakfast special, pancakes and sausage, grabbed a coffee to go and made a phone call to the sheriff's office for Leroy. Scotty said he was already at '*Nunamaker Stables*' and I could find him there.

I took a detour and drove by Dr. Jack Preston's office. Again, no one was there. It looked just as it did yesterday, no signs of life or activity.

'*Nunamaker Stables*' was located east of Hwy 70/79 on Graball Road. It was a huge property, containing numerous barns, stables, pastures and the Nunamaker residence.

The entrance road, the parking areas and the residence driveway were covered with vehicles. Fire trucks, ambulances, pickup trucks, police vehicles and panel trucks from the Madison County Crime Lab – it looked like a zoo and I needed to get in the middle of it!

Yellow crime tape surrounded the burned barn area, and stretched all the way around many of the surrounding buildings. Among all this confusion were several large tractors, which seemed to be removing the rubble and what was left of the animal carcasses. It was a terrible sight, and the misting rain made it worse.

I spotted Leroy talking with a man wearing a white lab coat and carrying a clipboard. I walked up just as he was finishing his conversation.

"Hi Carson," he quickly said to me. "I got your message. Is this a zoo or what?" Leroy looked around shaking his head.

"Looks that way to me," I said. "I'm not even sure where to start."

"Well, you'll need to decide that on your own. I'm headed up to the residence to talk with Susan Nunamaker; she arrived about an hour ago."

"What? You're kidding. You mean she just drove up and saw all this? She had no idea anything had happened here or to her husband?" I was confused.

"Evidently not," Leroy said. "She and their trainer, Justin Avery, have been in Florida running one of their horses at Gulfstream Park. I know it seems odd, but nobody knew how to contact them, none of the household help or none of the stable workers. I assume Aaron knew, but he wasn't around to ask!"

"Sounds strange, but I guess you'll know more after you talk with Susan," I said.

"Yep. Carson, what are your plans?" Leroy asked directly.

"I'm going to snoop around and talk with anybody I can find to talk with, in particular the part-time jockey, Eddie Merrick. Is that local vet, Doctor Preston, here? I really need to talk with him too."

"No, he isn't here and we can't find him," Leroy sounded frustrated. "I had to call in a veterinarian from Milan. Scotty and Jeff have checked his home, his office and every local beer joint he has been known to visit. Still no Dr. Preston."

"Guess that means you don't have any idea where I might look for him either– huh?" I asked.

"No, but talk with Scotty and Jeff, they might be able to point you in the right direction. I couldn't wait, I needed a veterinarian today."

"Why, the animals are obviously dead. What is the veterinarian going to do?" It was an honest question – I thought.

"Carson, you see that tall man with a suit and tie, the one walking through the rubble and ignoring the rain?" Leroy asked, pointing at a man standing in the middle of the burned barn area.

"Yes, so?" I asked.

"That's the insurance investigator, a Mr. Leonard Price. He is from Nashville. Forget the barn insurance, these thoroughbred horses were insured for over two million dollars! He's got his underwear in a twist, so I suggest you give him plenty of room and stay out of his way."

I was speechless and just stared at Leroy as I managed to utter, "Did you say two million dollars?"

"I did," Leroy repeated.

I caught my breath enough to finally say, "Shit. Well, we still just got dead horses here, what is he looking for?"

"All thoroughbred horses have a distinctive tattoo on the inside of their lip, he's looking for that. The problem is the condition of the carcasses; they are mostly burned to a crisp. He also knows that many uninsured horses were moved into the barn before the fire, so he could be looking at a saddle horse, not a thoroughbred. Unless he actually finds a tattoo, I expect this to be a long time getting settled."

"What a mess," I finally said.

"Yes, quite a mess," Leroy echoed. "Now, I'm going to talk with Susan Nunamaker. I don't want you talking with her, just yet. I'll meet you at Chiefs this evening and brief you on her story. Okay?"

"Yes, Leroy, that's fine. Can you tell me what that other entrance road is for, the one with the gate and lock? I saw it when I drove up earlier."

"That is the entrance used by the horse trailers and animal transportation. In fact, when Susan and that trainer arrived today, that's how they drove in. The trainer was driving a truck and pulling the horses; she was driving her car," Leroy answered.

"Two vehicles, isn't that odd?" I thought it was.

"Maybe," he said. "I'll ask her about it."

"Okay, see you at Chiefs later," I said to Leroy as he walked toward the Nunamaker residence.

This was a mess beyond most people's comprehension. The tractor was dragging out dead horse carcasses so the veterinarian and insurance investigator could examine them. The sight of this was bad enough, but the smell was worse! Following examination, the tractor would drag the carcasses to a large pit that had been dug in a pasture south of the barn area. I intended to take Leroy's advice, and stay away from Mr. Leonard Price, insurance investigator. He did not look like a happy man.

Standing next to one of the hay barns was a short man wearing work boots and leaning against a rake. I thought this might be a good place to start, so I walked over to where he was resting on the rake handle.

"Hello, my name is Carson Reno," I said politely. "I'm a private investigator looking into the murder of Aaron Nunamaker. Can we talk a minute?"

"I've already told the police everything I know, so why don't you just leave me alone. Okay?" He ignored me with his reply.

"Look, I'm not going to ask you police questions, they've already done that." I pulled a crisp $100 bill from my pocket, and folded it to get his attention. "My questions will be a little different and are probably worth more than theirs. Understand?"

"Let's go inside the barn," he said as he turned and walked inside one of the hay barns.

"Okay Mister, whatever your name is. Give me the hundred and we'll talk."

"The name's Carson Reno, and you'll get the hundred, but let's talk first. What is your name?" I asked, still holding the money where he could see it.

"Eddie Merrick, I work here. Sometimes I race, but mostly I just work with the horses here at the ranch."

"I know from your statement to the police, that you witnessed Todd Randal here the night of the murder and the fire. How often did Todd visit the stables?"

"Never, that I remember. But, he sure spent a lot of time up at the big house, mostly when Mr. Nunamaker was off racing somewhere," he chuckled.

"Really? Was Mrs. Nunamaker home during these visits?" I tried to not show my shock.

"How would I know, maybe he was visiting with one of the maids – you think?" he laughed at his own joke.

"Do you know Doctor Jack Preston, the vet?" I asked.

"Sure, who don't," he shrugged.

"When is the last time you saw him, and do you have any idea where he might be?" I asked, still showing the hundred.

"He was here the afternoon of the fire, and a couple of hours before Todd Randal showed up. Mr. Nunamaker had a mare in fold and I assume the doc was checking on her. They spent about an hour in the barn, but I was busy and never went over."

"And where might I find Dr. Preston?" I was still making sure he could see the hundred.

"Drunk, most likely. He hangs out at CC's poolroom in Humboldt and the poolroom in Trenton. I also heard him talk about some bar just outside Medina, a place I suspect he goes when he doesn't want any of his customers to find him."

"You know the name of that place in Medina?" I was interested.

"The *'DoLittle Inn'*, I think. I've never been there. Give me my hundred, this conversation is over." He was trying to leave.

70

"Just a couple more questions. Have you noticed any strange characters around the stables or barn?" I wanted my money's worth.

"What do you mean, 'strange'?" he asked staring at the hundred.

"People you didn't recognize. People that weren't necessarily 'horse people'."

"Yeah, all the time. Give me my hundred or I'm calling for a cop."

"Call away and I can keep the money, if you prefer," I threatened. "One more question. Have you seen a lot of movement of horses lately? I mean a lot of horses and trailers coming and going that wasn't normal?"

"Yes, yes," he stuttered. "Aaron was moving a lot of horse flesh lately, and I don't know to where. Now, do I get my money or not?"

I handed him the hundred and he quickly ran out of the barn. Eddie Merrick was a weasel of a guy and I wondered just how much truth that hundred had bought. Maybe he was just giving me answers I expected, but the answer about Todd being at the big house was NOT one I had expected!

~

I had seen enough at *'Nunamaker Stables'* and my next stop was the sheriff's office. I noticed the 59 Chevrolet Impala behind me when I left *'Nunamaker Stables'* and it followed when I reached the main highway. As before, he stayed about a quarter of a mile back and only seemed interested in following, not talking.

At Bailey Park, I took the north entrance and slowed to see if he followed, he did. When I parked at the pavilion, they drove by slowly and stopped before exiting back onto the main road. I took my .38 from the glove box, placed it in my waistband and walked toward their car. They didn't move.

I walked up to the driver's side and the window was down. "Excuse me," I asked. "Could either of you tell me how to get to the cemetery?"

The driver gave me a dirty look before he spoke. "Listen asshole, this ain't traveler's aide. You need directions, visit a gas station."

"I don't need directions; I just wanted to make sure you knew how to get there. Because, if you keep following me, someone will need to tell your next of kin where to find you."

He reached for his weapon, but I already had mine at the window. "You wanna see if yours is bigger than mine?" I asked politely.

The passenger spoke; he was a little nicer. "Look mister, we're not following you. That's just what it seemed like, it's a mistake that's all. We're not looking for trouble."

"Then what are you looking for? I know damn well you're following me, and this isn't the first time. I'll tell you what, I'm headed to the sheriff's office, so why not follow me and we can finish this discussion there?"

Without comment, the driver started the car and quickly drove out of the park and back onto the main road. I got the plate 1-R3429.

~

Jeff was manning the desk when I walked into the sheriff's office.

"Hey, Jeff. Have you been out to the Nunamaker place?" I asked.

"Sure have, and what a zoo. You need to see Leroy? If so, he's not here." Jeff was being helpful.

"Not really, just checking in. You guys got anything new on the cause of death?"

"Ha!" Jeff laughed. "That's not likely to change, a bullet through the ticker, however, we have no slug, it went all the way through the body. But, we do have a spent cartridge in Todd's rifle, still in the chamber. A slam dunk if you ask me."

"Anything from the insurance guy?" I was probing for information.

"Yeah, Leroy radioed and says he had no positive identification on any of the horses, meaning he can't verify that any thoroughbreds actually died in the fire - this should get interesting."

"I believe it will," I told Jeff. "What about Susan Nunamaker? I understand she finally showed up today."

"She did, and claimed to know nothing about what had happened. Leroy's got us checking on her alibi. She claims she was at Gulfstream Track in Hallendale Beach, Florida at a horse race. We're working on that now," Jeff added.

"When you get time, can you run a plate for me, a Shelby County tag?" I asked.

"Sure, as long as you aren't in a hurry. What's the number?"

"1-R3429, and I'm in no hurry; I'll check back tomorrow."

"We'll probably have it in a few hours, depending upon how busy the DMV is. Do you need to see Todd Randal? Leroy said to let you talk to him whenever you needed," Jeff offered.

"No, not now," I said. "Jack Logan should be here this afternoon and I know he will want to talk with Todd." I started to leave, then turned around. "Hey, do you guys have any idea where I might find Dr. Jack Preston?"

"Nope, Scotty and I have searched everywhere, and no luck. We know his usual hangouts and came up a zero. We also checked his office and house, of course. He's off drunk somewhere; he'll show up, always does."

I left with a lot more information than I had when I walked in there. It was good, but I still needed to find Dr. Jack Preston.

More Information

*M*y first stop was CC Burgess' Pool Room. Billy Wayne was behind the counter, as he always was. I took a stool and ordered a draft beer.

"Carson Reno," he said delivering my beer with a laugh. "What brings you to CC's poolroom? We don't have any women, we don't have any whiskey and we don't have any music. You lost?"

"Probably, but I'm looking for someone and thought I might find him in here."

"And who might that be?" he asked, while wiping off the counter.

"Dr. Jack Preston. Have you seen him lately?"

"Not in a few days. Guess he is soaking it up somewhere else. That guy makes me glad I don't own an animal. He's a drunk, and probably kills more with his treatment than he saves. If you need a vet, I suggest you find somebody else," Billy Wayne laughed.

"I don't need his services; I just need to talk to him. You ever heard of a place in Medina called the *'DoLittle Inn'*?"

"Sure, it's on the highway between Medina and Three Way, but I don't recommend it."

"Yeah? Why?" I asked.

"Carson, it is a rough joint. Even the police don't go in there, and you're crazy if YOU do, that's why." Billy Wayne was serious.

"Okay. We'll see. Thanks for advice," I said as I got up to leave.

"We'll take up a collection and send flowers!" Billy Wayne yelled as I walked out the door.

I wish he hadn't said that. Billy Wayne's high recommendation of the *'DoLittle Inn'* didn't add to my anticipation of having to make that visit. Maybe I wouldn't need to. Maybe I could find the drunk, Dr. Preston, somewhere else.

~

My third visit to Dr. Preston's office produced the same results, nothing.

Hoping to avoid the *'DoLittle Inn'*, I decided to give the poolroom in Trenton a try. Maybe I would get lucky.

Runt's PoolRoom in Trenton was located just off the town square. I had been there once or twice in my younger days, but really didn't expect I would see anyone I knew. I was wrong.

Sitting on a raised stool next to the stove, smoking a Camel and watching a big money pool game was Richard P. 'Dick' Valentine.

Dick Valentine was the former Humboldt Chief of Police. He and Leroy Epsee had run for the job of Gibson County Sheriff a few years ago. Leroy's platform promise was to clean up the city of Humboldt and that included getting rid of Dick Valentine as Chief of Police. When Valentine learned what Leroy was planning, he decided to join in the race for sheriff, too.

It was a tough campaign and close vote, but Leroy prevailed. Then he set out to fulfill his promise of getting rid of Valentine. It wasn't difficult.

Valentine was on the take from almost everybody. If you were a bad guy, it wasn't hard to get by with almost anything in Humboldt. All you needed to do was make sure Dick Valentine got his cut. Illegal gambling, prostitution, bootleggers and even an occasional moon-shiner worked under the watchful eyes of Richard P. 'Dick' Valentine. They were known on the street as 'Valentine's Boys' and nobody interfered with their activities.

Leroy helped get a new mayor elected and finally Valentine and most of his police force were put on the street. The new chief, Raymond Griggs, and Leroy are doing a good job of putting most of the 'Valentine Boys' out of business and in jail. They still had work to do, but the community is now a much better and safer place to live and work.

Valentine never went to jail and I never knew what had happened to him. Now, here he was sitting on a stool watching a pool game in 'Runts' Pool Room in Trenton.

I took the seat next to Dick Valentine, not saying anything. Dick turned, looked at me and then turned back to watch the pool game – he said nothing.

After a few minutes, he snuffed out his Camel and quickly lit another. Then, without looking at me he said, "Reno, why are you in this poolroom and why are you sitting on that stool next to me?"

"I'm looking for somebody," I responded. "Why, is this seat taken?"

"Well, whoever you're looking for isn't here," he said, still watching the pool game.

"How do you know that?" I asked curiously.

"Because if they were here, you would be sitting next to them and talking to them, not me." He had a point.

"I'm looking for Dr. Jack Preston. You know where I might find him?" I asked.

Still watching the pool game he said, "You might have to get in line, seems like everybody is looking for Dr. Jack Preston."

"Oh, yeah? Who is 'everybody else'?"

"A couple of tough guys from Memphis. They didn't say, but I suspect they work for Steve Carrollton, the Mafia guy. You know him?" He was still talking without looking at me.

"Sure, I know him. Did these two guys have a name?" I asked.

"Unless their parents were real assholes, I'm sure they gave them a name," he answered sarcastically.

"Well, did these two guys happen to give YOU their names?" Getting this guy to talk was like pulling teeth.

He put out one Camel, and quickly lit another. "They didn't give it, but I knew it anyway."

"Will you share the names with me, or do I need to pay for that information?"

"You don't owe me anything, Mr. Carson Reno, and I don't want to be on some paid snitch list. Their names are James Henry King and Johnie Gibson – two guys you really don't want to mess with." He was still watching the pool game, and it was almost like he was talking to himself.

"Oh, yeah, how do you know?" I asked.

"Let's just leave it at 'I know'," he said. "I might have had some business dealings with them in the past. Trust me, don't mess with them."

"Okay Dick, I believe you," I said with some frustration. "Now back to where we started. Do you know where I can find Dr. Jack Preston?"

"No, but if I did, I would have told them. They asked first. I don't, so I guess everybody is still looking. I haven't seen him in over a week, and he was drunk then. Come to think of it, I can't remember ever seeing him when he wasn't drunk."

"You think I might find him if I looked at the *'DoLittle Inn'*?"

Finally, Dick Valentine turned and looked at me. "Reno, unless you got bigger balls than I think you do, you'll stay away from that place. People have been known to go in there and never come out – understand?" Then he turned back to watching the pool game.

"You didn't answer me. Do you think I might find him at the *'DoLittle Inn'*?" I asked again.

"How should I know. Maybe you and the Mafia tough guys should team up and go there together – it would be safer that way!"

While he was so talkative, I thought I would try to get all the information I could. "Alright Dick, you've made your point. What do you know about Aaron Nunamaker?"

"He's dead," he said while lighting another Camel.

"Is that all you know?"

He turned and looked at me again. "What is this, some kind of a quiz show? He's dead. Somebody shot him and burned his barn and his horses along with his corpse. That's what I know." He turned back to the pool game.

"Any idea why somebody might have done this to him?" I asked.

"Yeah, lots of ideas. You wanna hear them?"

"I sure do," I said trying to hide my enthusiasm.

Richard P. 'Dick' Valentine continued to stare at the ongoing pool game while he talked. He never looked at me.

Dick said that Nunamker was in real deep with the mob, mostly from gambling. Sometimes on his horses and sometimes on somebody else's, but almost always losing. He was in so deep that the Mafia was actually controlling '*Nunamaker Stables*' – and that wasn't good. The mob was selling off his assets to cover his debts, and that included some fine horses. What the mob couldn't sell in the states, they were sending to South America for racing or for stud with the majority going to Columbia for a Julio Escobar. Escobar had his own thoroughbred operation in Bogota, bought mostly with blood and drugs.

To stay afloat, Nunamaker was cutting a lot of corners, which included false stud certifications, fake records and using unqualified stock for breeding. He was on a short rope without a knot at the end. When he fell, he would fall hard.

Valentine speculated the fire was meant to cover something else, not just his murder. And he also speculated that probably a heavy insurance policy was in place to cover the loss.

When he heard they found a body in the barn, he figured it would have been Susan Nunamaker or Todd Randal or perhaps both. Their activities weren't hidden from many eyes, and those included Aaron Nunamaker's.

Richard P. 'Dick' Valentine stopped talking just a quickly as he had started.

"Do you think the mob might have bumped him off, maybe your two friends King and Gibson?" I asked, hoping to get him started again.

"Why kill the goose?" he added. "Unless the goose had tried a doublecross, they had no reason. They planned to milk him for everything, and then walk away."

"You used to be a cop. Who do you think did it?"

"Todd Randal," he answered. "He's under arrest, isn't he? They fight, perhaps over Susan, and Nunamaker ends up dead."

"Why burn the barn?" I asked.

"I don't know – ask Randal. Or better yet, ask Leroy. How is my buddy Leroy doing? Still cleaning up the streets?" he said sarcastically.

"You mean you don't know?"

"No, and I don't care. This conversation is over," Valentine said as he stood up and walked toward the back of the poolroom. Yes, the conversation was over.

~

I left Runt's Pool Room with a lot of information I didn't expect to get when I walked in there. That was good, but I still needed to talk with Dr. Jack Preston. I pointed the Ford toward Medina.

I'm hardheaded, but two people had warned me to stay out of the *'DoLittle Inn'*. I wasn't sure what I was going to do, but at least I wanted to drive by the place and see what everybody was afraid of.

The *'DoLittle Inn'* Bar

The *'DoLittle Inn'* didn't impress me as one of those places you would find on everyone's 'must see' list. I parked out front and thought this one over; maybe it would be better not to do this alone – I decided to wait.

There were only nine vehicles in the parking lot, two trucks and one car along with 6 motorcycles. I wrote the tag numbers and would have Leroy's office check them out. If Dr. Jack Preston was among them, I could come back later.

~

I dropped the tag numbers off with Scotty at the Sheriff's office and learned that Jack Logan was already in town. He had left word that he would be visiting with Judy Strong this afternoon and planned to meet me for dinner at Chiefs. I also got the information I had requested on the 59 Chevrolet Impala. It was registered to Capital Loan and Pawn, Beale Street, Memphis - Steve Carrollton's office address.

Carrollton's Office Beale Street Memphis

~

I drove by Pullums and picked up 2 pounds of Bar –B-Q plus the trimmings for dad and myself. Pullums had the best Bar-B-Q anywhere east of Memphis, except maybe Bozos, but they didn't count. Bozos is a restaurant where you went to eat, most people used Pullums for take out.

Dad and I could have lunch while I caught up on the local gossip from mother. A few hours with Mom and Dad would give me time to think about my next move.

Pullums Bar-B-Q

The visit at home was typical. Dad had been traveling with his TVA job and mother was full of useless information and gossip that I really didn't need to know. Dad and I had a beer and barbecue sandwich while mother filled my ear. I was listening, but my thoughts were on the events of the day. I needed to catch up with Leroy and his visit with Susan Nunamaker, and I also needed to bring Jack Logan up to speed with my progress so far.

We finished our Bar-B-Q and I said good-by – promising to call later. Then I pointed the Ford toward Chiefs. I'm sure I had messages.

~

Something was definitely wrong when I walked in Chiefs. It took me a moment to figure out the problem, and I'm not sure why it took me so long. THE JUKEBOX WASN'T PLAYING!

Sitting on the floor in front of the jukebox was a man wearing gray overalls with a label on his back that read 'Dan's Music Box Repair'. He had already removed the front of the music machine and had most of its internal parts spread over the dining room floor when I walked in. Nickie was obviously, supervising. She had her hands on her hips and spouting constant instructions to this poor repairman. I certainly hope he gets it repaired before she really gets serious about it! The death of this jukebox would be something that would put her in mourning for the foreseeable future.

I quietly slipped to a barstool and asked Barbie to bring me a Jack and Coke. Nickie was so engrossed in the jukebox problem, she wouldn't have known if the building was on fire!

"Hey Nickie," I yelled. "We can give that thing a proper burial? If you want, I'll even send flowers."

She wasn't amused. "It isn't dead, Carson," she quietly said. "It is just sick and this nice man is here to make it feel better. And, as I have already told him, he has another hour to perform his surgery or he will need to bring in a substitute. Right, Mr. Repairman?" she said glaring at the man on the floor.

He didn't answer and now had his head completely inside that machine. I'm sure Nickie had been giving him instructions since he walked in the door.

Nickie walked over to my barstool. "Don't get your hopes up, Mr. Reno. We'll have music for our night crowd; that is a promise."

"Okay, but can you break away from this surgery long enough to give me my messages?" I asked politely.

"Sure, let me get my order pad," she said as she went behind the bar and retrieved her notes. "First, you need to call your associate, Joe Richardson. He will be in his office. Second, Jack Logan will meet you here for dinner at 7:00. Third, Leroy wants to talk with you, and you should call him at his office. And finally, Elizabeth Teague called and you should call her at her Memphis apartment. That's it," she added.

"Thank you, you are a great secretary." That was a compliment, I thought.

"Go to hell, Carson - I am not a secretary," she snapped. "So go make your phone calls and don't forget that message from Miss Teague. I am not responsible for what you do with these messages, I only take and deliver them."

I left well enough alone and went outside to use the pay phone.

My first call was to Liz. She had just gotten back from an overseas flight, and had a short trip for tomorrow, but would be back in Memphis tomorrow night. I told her I would call, and to expect me in Memphis tomorrow evening.

My second call was to Leroy. He was in his office, and I asked if he could join Jack and me for dinner at 7:00. He agreed.

The last call was to Joe. I waited to call him last because I expected it to be a long call – it was.

He had spent a lot of boring and unproductive hours following Farnsworth, until yesterday when Joe had followed him to West Memphis, Arkansas. There, he witnessed a parking lot meeting between Farnsworth and an unknown man. They sat in Farnsworth's car for about 15 minutes, then the unknown man got out of the car and entered his own car – Joe followed the unknown man.

The unknown man drove only a few miles and then stopped at a bar. Joe got his license number and immediately took it to Larry Parker for identification.

The car belonged to a previously convicted third-rate burglar named Sammy 'the shiv' Thompson. According to his nickname, Sammy was known to carry a knife during his activities.

"Joe," I said, "that is terrific investigation. You have done a great job. Now I need you to do a few more things."

"Point me in the right direction Carson, I'm ready." You could hear the excitement in his voice.

"Since Farnsworth has been sticking close to home, I want you to get the names and background of all his neighbors. In particular, any unattached females that might live within a walking, or sneaking, distance from his house. My guess is that Sammy Thompson had the jewels, meaning the transfer back to Farnsworth and payoff happened during this parking lot meeting. If it did, then we can probably expect some of these items to show up somewhere soon, and my bet is on some lady he knows."

"Got it," Joe said. "Anything else?"

"Yes, and this concerns another case. I want you to find out where Todd Randal stayed and slept during his last weekend's visit to Hot Springs. You need to check every hotel, motel, rental trailer park, house, outhouse, hen house, whore house or anywhere you can rent sleeping space. He stayed somewhere, and I want to know where that was. Can you make that happen?" I asked.

"No problem," he responded quickly. "Will I see you soon or do you want me to call you with what I find?"

"Call me, but I expect to see you sometime tomorrow. If my hunch is correct, we will be able to quickly turn this Farnsworth case back over to Black Diamond and collect our money. Then you can help me with this fiasco I'm involved in up here in Humboldt."

I hung up and walked back into Chiefs – just in time to hear my worst nightmare come back to life. The jukebox was fixed!

I found my barstool and watched Nickie dance over to me as some unknown country song filled the bar with its usual melody.

"See," she said giggling. "I told you it wasn't dead, just sick. I know that makes you happy."

"Nickie, you are precious, I'm glad you are happy now. I know you were concerned about its health," I laughed.

"Yes I was. Can I get you something to eat or drink?" she said while still dancing.

"I'm going to my room and freshen up. Leroy, Jack and I will be having dinner here later. Make sure Ronnie has some good steaks. I know I'm buying," I added.

"Will do," she said – still dancing!

~

Jack was already in a booth when I walked back in Chiefs. I had barely gotten seated when Leroy pulled into the parking lot and quickly joined us.

We ordered drinks and I shared the story of my visit with Richard Valentine at the Trenton poolroom. Jack listened intently and didn't ask questions. Leroy seemed a little annoyed about my conversation. I understood.

When I finished I looked at Jack and said, "Our client is not telling us the truth. I don't know what he told you today, but unless it is something different than we have already heard, most of it is a lie. He's lying for a reason; we need to figure out what that reason is. But, based upon my conversations with Billy Grayson, I absolutely believe Todd did not kill Nunamaker; however, I think he has a good idea who did. Obviously he is scared, but I don't understand why he would be protecting somebody. He's the one in jail and headed toward a trial for murder."

"Carson, his story didn't change," Jack said. "I didn't confront him with any of this information, because I didn't have it, but I will tomorrow. Maybe he'll change his story, we'll see."

Then I looked at Leroy, "What was Susan Nunamaker's story?"

"She says she left on Thursday with Justin Avery, the trainer, and they were in Hallandale Beach until they returned on Tuesday," he answered.

"And Justin Avery's story?" I asked.

"He backed it up 100%. He said they left on Thursday, drove to Florida and raced their horse. Then they returned on Tuesday, arriving when we saw them."

"He's lying," I said. "And if he's lying, she's lying. Why did she have her car?" I asked Leroy.

"She claims she had some errands to run and left her car in town. We checked, but can't verify that; however, it doesn't seem too strange," Leroy added.

"You did verify their stay in Florida?" I asked Leroy.

"Yes, smart ass. We do know how to do our job," he snapped.

"I know," I said. "Forget that question. Does anybody know where we can find Dr. Jack Preston? I know he has something to add."

Both Jack and Leroy shook their heads, then Leroy spoke. "What we do know is that somebody broke into his office. They trashed the place, but without him, we don't know if anything was stolen."

"When did that happen?" I asked Leroy.

"Sometime last night, one of his customers reported it this morning and Jeff investigated. They kicked in a back door and tore the place up pretty good. But, until we find him, we don't know if anything was taken."

"What do you know about the *'DoLittle Inn'*?" I asked Leroy.

"I know you better stay away – we do! If Dr. Preston is there, and I doubt it, he's crazier than I think he is."

"Leroy, you're not the first person to tell me that, believe me. But I intend to find him, one way or another."

"Carson," Jack asked. "When are you going to get your new associate up here to help?"

"Soon, probably later this week," I answered. "I'm going back to Memphis tomorrow and hopefully wrap up another case. I'll be bringing him back, probably."

"Good idea," Jack acknowledged. "And if you decide to visit this *'DoLittle Inn'*, he can help pick up your pieces!"

"My thoughts exactly," Leroy added with a chuckle.

"Okay guys, I get the message," I muttered. "Leroy, tell me about this jockey and horse that were victims of the hit and run?"

"His name was Harry Smiley, and I don't know the horse's name! Anyway, they were run down with one of the '*Nunamaker Stables*' trucks – apparently stolen. We found the truck; a 1960 Chevrolet abandoned about a mile from the accident. No clues, no witnesses and we've gotten nowhere with our investigations."

"Did you talk with his wife – family?" I asked.

"Scotty did. He talked with his wife. She had nothing to add," Leroy said.

"Okay, I may revisit that. Meanwhile, I need Jack to drill down with Todd. Everybody is lying and I'm not sure when I hear the truth and when I don't. I know some pieces, but there are some large holes in everybody's story. Maybe I'll know more when I get back from Memphis," I said to everyone.

We had a few more drinks, then dinner and spent the evening discussing our various theories regarding the murder of Aaron Nunamaker. I have some real ideas, but it is extremely difficult when everybody is lying, especially the person you are working for, and the one you are tying to prove innocent.

Everyone made it an early evening and I prepared for my trip back to Memphis tomorrow.

Elliot Farnsworth

I had several stops to make before leaving town and it was almost 11 before I finally grabbed my coffee to go and pointed the Ford toward the sheriff's office. First, I needed to talk with Scotty about his conversation with the dead jockey's wife.

Scotty was at the front desk when I walked in. "Scotty, you got a minute?" I asked.

"Sure, anything for you Carson," he pushed his paperwork aside. "What's up?"

"Tell me about your interview with Harry Smiley's wife."

"Not much to tell," he said. "She had nothing to add about the hit and run. She had no idea who might have done it or why. I just asked the usual questions and made my report for Leroy. It was, of course, a difficult time for her, plus she had a house full of curtain climbers and they had most of her attention."

"Curtain climbers?" I questioned.

"You know, little kids. There must have been 3 or 4 crawling around the house. I don't know how or why people would have that many kids so close together, and none of them were old enough to walk, I don't think," he said shaking his head.

"What is her address?" I asked. "I'm going to pay her a visit before I head back to Memphis. We know a little more now than we did then, and perhaps she has moved on with her grief."

"I'll get the address, but I wouldn't trouble myself with her grief," he said frankly.

"What do you mean?"

"She wasn't grieving, that's what I mean. She didn't seem the least bit upset that her husband had just been run over and killed. It seemed odd, but I don't know anything about their personal life."

"Interesting," I said to myself.

Scotty handed me a slip of paper with the name and address. I pointed the Ford in that direction.

Jack and Linda Smiley
212 McKnight Street
Humboldt, TN

There was nothing special about 212 McKnight Street. A small wooden house with an old pickup parked in the dirt driveway.

A petite woman with long brown hair that needed attention answered the door after my first knock. She was wearing an apron over a simple blue cotton dress. I could hear kids crying in the background and the odor of dirty diapers made me backup when she opened the door!

"What do you want?" she asked in a very unpleasant tone.

"My name is Carson Reno, and I'm looking for Linda Smiley. Are you Linda?"

"No, I ain't Linda and she ain't here," she snapped.

"Well, do you know where I might reach her?" I asked. "It's important that I speak with her, it's about her husband's death."

"You the insurance man? You got more money?" she said with excitement.

"No, I'm not an insurance man and I.....,"she interrupted me before I could finish.

"Then go away. I'm her sister and I don't know where she is. She took that money and left me with these babies. She said there would be a man with more money in a day or two and I was to keep it for myself. So, if you ain't that man with that money, just go away," she replied in the same unpleasant tone.

"I'm sorry, but I have no idea what you are talking about," I said.

She slammed the door in my face!

Now, that was just about the strangest conversation I have ever had! I got back in the Ford knowing less than I did when knocked on the door, if that was possible.

However, I was smart enough to know that no insurance had paid any death benefits, and I wasn't sure they had even put Harry Smiley in the ground yet! If somebody was delivering cash to 212 McKnight Street, it definitely wasn't an insurance adjuster.

Before leaving town, I stopped back by the sheriff's office and told the story to Scotty. I asked him to brief Leroy and I would call him later from Memphis. I never did.

~

It was mid-afternoon when I finally walked into the Peabody lobby and waved at Marcie.

"Marcie," I shouted. "Is Joe here?"

"Yep, he's in his office. I'll tell him you're here."

Before I got to my desk, Joe walked in with a smile from ear to ear. I could tell he had good news; it was hard for him to hide it!

"Carson, you are one smart detective. Now I understand why Rita wanted me to work for you and not some of those other deadbeats. How do you know these things?" he was excited.

"Joe, before we start swapping spit and slapping each other on the back, why don't you calm down? Please have a seat and tell me why all the excitement."

"I found Farnsworth's girlfriend. You told me to look around his neighborhood for a possible connection; well I found it – right next door! Mrs. Theodore Faulkner, a widow, lives next door to our Mr. Elliot Farnsworth. She has been widowed slightly longer than Farnsworth and is reported to be moderately wealthy."

"Okay, but how do you know she's his girlfriend? You got anything else?" I asked finding a seat behind my desk.

"Well for one, I checked and they have an adjoining gate at the back of their properties. Meaning that trips could be made between the residences and no one would ever know."

"Okay, you're getting warm, but anything else?" I continued.

"Yep, one other small clue, they have reservations for 8 tonight at the Starlight!" Joe was grinning ear to ear.

"What?" I almost fell out of my chair.

"Dinner, drinks and dancing tonight – 8 o'clock at the Starlight Lounge. Reservations confirmed." He was smiling so big I was afraid he would hurt himself!

"Joe, how do you know this?" I was almost speechless.

"My sister is in town and we were visiting with Rita last night. I was telling her about the insurance investigation and somewhere the name Farnsworth came up. Rita remembered taking a reservation for someone by that name. So she checked, and 'bingo' we have a match!"

"Joe, you are good! I'm not paying you enough!" I said without thinking.

"You're not paying me at all," he said, "but that's alright. That's the deal we made, I'm not complaining."

"I guarantee you a bonus, compliments of 'Black Diamond Insurance'. You earned it," I promised.

"Thanks. So, what do we do now?" He was still excited.

"We're going to the Starlight Lounge tonight. Call Rita and have her reserve us a table next to Mr. Farnsworth and his lady friend. I'll probably bring Liz, so make it for three. All we need to do is get a positive identification on any piece of that jewelry, and our job is finished. We'll make a full report to Bert Sappington and turn it back over to Black Diamond."

"What if she isn't wearing any of the jewelry?" he asked sheepishly.

"Then I'll eat my hat," I exclaimed. "He's been waiting to get those jewels from that West Memphis burglar and now he has set up a special occasion with Mrs. 'what's her name' to let her show them off. I don't think we need to worry, just make sure you know the jewels well enough to spot them. Okay?"

"Okay, but you don't wear a hat!" he laughed. "I'll spend a couple of hours reviewing the photos. Should I call Larry Parker?"

"No, not necessary, we'll leave that to Bert Sappington. What did you find out about Todd Randal and his housing arrangements in Hot Springs?"

"Nothing yet, Carson, I'm waiting on a couple of return phone calls, and I should know something by this evening."

"Good. And if this Farnsworth thing goes as I expect, you'll need to pack a bag."

"Oh, yeah, where am I going?" Joe asked excitedly.

"Humboldt. I'll give you the details tonight, but plan on it."

Joe went back into his office and I called Liz. She answered on the first ring.

"This better be Carson Reno, I'm not taking any other calls," she said in one of her mysterious voices.

"Were you expecting someone else?" I asked.

"None of your business, but it is nice to hear your voice. Are you in town, I hope?"

"I am in town and would like to get 'out on the town' tonight, are you available?"

"Available isn't a word I like, but I would love to share a drink and dinner with you tonight. Does that make me 'available'?" she said with a giggle.

"It does, and I have just the plan. I have a little work to do tonight, but we can share that drink and dinner while I'm working." I didn't think she was going to like that statement. She didn't.

"Carson Reno, I am not 'sharing' my evening with your work. Either you work, or you play – make up your mind!"

"Listen, it isn't a big deal, and I'll explain it to you tonight. Joe Richardson will be joining us for dinner and our work shouldn't take more than a couple of hours." I was just digging myself into a deeper hole.

"So, now you're not only working, but I must share my evening with Joe Richardson! Why don't you just call me back when you have more time?"

"Look Liz, don't get so out of sorts. I'll make it up to you, promise. Pick me up at my apartment at 7 and I'll explain everything. Okay?"

"You'd better, or no scrambled eggs for you tomorrow. I'll see you at 7." She hung up.

I must learn to do better. That was just no way to ask someone for a date, and I'm surprised she agreed to pick me up. I'll make it up to her, somehow.

~

At 6:55 that familiar red corvette pulled into my apartment parking lot. Liz hopped out. First she tossed me the keys and then gave me a big hug and kiss. Maybe all has been forgiven?

She's wearing a striking red outfit and is simply gorgeous, as usual. The customary high heels give her a couple of inches on me, but I know she likes it that way. It was my task to drive this four speed, 327 cubic inch monster, while dealing with the distraction of her riding in the passenger seat. Not an easy task, trust me.

I explained the whole Farnsworth case during our drive to the Starlight Lounge. While she was disappointed that I was working and that our evening would be at the Starlight, I think there was a small level of excitement. Liz wouldn't admit it, but she did like the intrigue of my work – I think.

As usual, Rita greeted us at the door and we were quickly seated at our table. Joe was already there, but Farnsworth and his date had not yet arrived.

"Is there going to be any 'gun-play' tonight?" Liz asked us both.

"I sure hope not," I said laughing and shaking my head. "This Farnsworth character isn't the 'gun-play' type, and I'm sure Rita wouldn't appreciate it. So, let's have drinks, dinner and some dances, my plans are for Farnsworth to never know we are here. We just need to confirm the presence of some jewelry and our job is complete."

"Gee whiz, Carson," she said. "If we're going to catch bad guys, there should be some excitement, right?"

"Wrong!" I answered strongly.

While we had drinks, I brought Joe up to speed on the Aaron Nunamaker's murder and where I had taken it to at this point. I told him to plan on meeting at the office in the morning, and we would discuss travel to Humboldt.

Elizabeth listened, but didn't seem to be interested in our conversation. However, she was interested in all the odd and strange customers gathered at the Starlight. I'm sure Elizabeth Teague had never witnessed anything quite like it; this just wasn't her type of place.

Finally Liz said, "Carson, I forgot to tell you. I am traveling to Humboldt tomorrow. Mary Ellen is hosting a benefit for the homeless at the Country Club and I promised to help her with the arrangements. Didn't I hear you say you were going back tomorrow too?"

"Yes, I am." I answered almost like a question.

"Good. Then you will escort me to the benefit. I don't have the details, but will let you know when I do." That was not a request, but an order. I said nothing.

Finally at 8:15 a stately looking elderly gentleman and an attractive silver hared lady were seated at the table we knew to be reserved for Farnsworth. Joe nodded, letting me know that this was Mr. Elliot Farnsworth and Mrs. Theodore Faulkner.

Joe had a perfect view of the lady and I gave him a questionable look, wanting to know if he had spotted any of the missing jewelry. Joe touched his neck letting me know she was wearing one of the missing necklaces – we had him!

Then Joe touched his finger telling me she was wearing one of the missing rings, then Joe touched his chest letting me know she was wearing a missing broach! I held my hand up and told him to stop. Farnsworth had out done himself – surely he was going to get laid tonight! But it was an expensive date!

I told Joe to just forget them; we had all we needed. We ordered dinner and made small talk for the rest of the evening. My highlight was a dance with Liz to my favorite song – 'At Last' sung by Etta James. Damn I love that song!

We left at 11 and I told Joe to meet me at the office early tomorrow. Of course he knew that meant 10 or 10:30 – naturally.

Liz and I spent the rest of the evening at the 'Down Under', drinking wine and catching up on where we had last left off. I had made certain my apartment was stocked with eggs, so we took an early elevator home.

~

When I reached the office next morning, Joe had already called Bert Sappington and they were just waiting on me.

Bert listened to our information and we quickly put this case in the books. Drake Detective Agency would be drawing a nice check from Black Diamond Insurance. Damn, this was good work when you could get it!

~

After Bert Sappington left I asked, "Joe, what have you learned about Todd Randal and his housing in Hot Springs?"

"I got confirmation this morning. Mr. and Mrs. Randal spent the weekend at the Park Hotel in Hot Springs and they checked out Saturday morning."

Park Hotel Hot Springs, Arkansas

"Mr. and Mrs. Randal? This guy isn't married! On Saturday? He said he left on Friday night!" I was pissed and it showed.

"Carson, I don't know what to tell you. This is real information and confirmed," Joe added.

"Joe," I said, "I want you to grab your clothes and drive your car to Humboldt. Find Chiefs, introduce yourself to Nickie, and I'll be only a few minutes behind you. Also, stop by the sheriff's office and tell them you are in town. We'll meet at Chiefs this evening and discuss plans."

Joe left and I just sat for a minute. So far, most everything Todd Randal had told us was a lie. If I didn't really believe him to be innocent, I would have folded up my tent and taken it to the house. The next few days were going to be interesting, I promise.

~

I was deep in thought about my next move when my office door opened. In walked James Henry King.

"You have an appointment?" I was startled and asked as I looked up.

"Yep," he said, pulling a pistol from a shoulder holster.

I've noticed that guns always look bigger when they're pointed at you – this one was no exception. James Henry King was holding a .45 automatic and it was aimed at my head.

I raised my hands and said, "Hey, we're easy to please. If you need an appointment that bad, I'm sure I can work you in!"

"You just did. Now, I need you to put your hands down and quietly walk in front of me. Don't talk to anyone and don't stop until I tell you to. Understand?" He was not kidding.

"I do understand. Where are we going? It might make it easier if you told me," I said as I stepped toward my office door.

"To the parking garage, and as I said, don't speak to anyone and don't stop until I tell you." He was pushing me toward the exit.

The doorman spoke to both of us as we walked out the southwest entrance door. As instructed, I said nothing, and it was only a short walk across the guest arrival driveway to the Peabody Hotel Parking garage. I'm sure no one, other than the doorman, saw us leave the hotel.

Parking Garage Peabody Hotel

The man behind me with the big gun was James Henry King - one of the two Mafia associates that had followed me in the 59 Chevrolet Impala. He was also one of the two guys Dick Valentine had warned me about. It was obvious this was not a social visit.

As we entered the covered garage, I once again saw the black 59 Chevy Impala. And leaning up against the hood was the other member of that duo, Johnie Gibson.

Parked next to the Chevrolet was a 59 Cadillac Limousine with the engine running.

The .45 once again appeared in James Henry King's hand, and he opened the rear passenger side door. "Get in," he said with a jester of the .45.

I took a seat next to the door and glanced at a big man setting on the bench seat across from the bar, he was in the process of making himself a drink. I was looking at a well-dressed and well-tanned Hispanic man with a large unlit cigar in the corner of his mouth. He was middle aged with thinning dark hair and probably fifty pounds overweight. Obviously, he appreciated jewelry, because he was wearing plenty. He had rings on most fingers and a large gold cross dangling just inside his partially unbuttoned white shirt.

"Can I offer you a drink Mr. Reno?" he asked.

I shook my head and didn't speak. I was busy surveying my situation and contemplating making a run for it. James Henry King and Johnie Gibson were out of my sight and I had no idea where they might be. I also could not see the limo driver, but I was sure someone was sitting in the driver's seat.

There would not be any Peabody Hotel Garage workers present, only routine runners dispatched by the doorman to handle valet parking, so I expected I was alone with my captors.

"Mr. Reno, my name is Julio Escobar, and I require a favor from you," he said while sipping his freshly made drink.

I didn't acknowledge his comment and simply looked at him without any expression.

"I understand you have been employed to solve the terrible murder of Mr. Aaron Nunamaker and many of his prized thoroughbreds. I appreciate the difficulty of your task and wish you luck in your efforts."

I didn't speak.

"Mr. Reno, prior to his death, Mr. Nunamaker owed me and my organization a lot of money. However, thanks to my associates and some of their friends, we have managed to recover most of what was owed, but another problem has surfaced."

I didn't speak.

"Some very important documents that belong to me have disappeared. These are documents that are necessary for me to completely recover my losses from Mr. Nunamaker. It seems that an animal doctor has taken these documents to prevent me from moving my recovered assets to my natural country, Columbia. I can't imagine why he would do this, but it has happened. Do you understand, Mr. Reno?"

I didn't speak.

"My associates will soon find this animal doctor and we will then no longer need to have any dealings with you and your Humboldt friends. I hope that day comes soon, but I'm troubled because my associates tell me you are also looking for this animal doctor. Is that true?"

I didn't speak.

"Very well, I see you chose not to have conversation with me, that doesn't matter. What I require is that you stop searching for this animal doctor, and please let my associates handle finding him. After we recover my documents, you are welcome to him. And hopefully he will help you in resolving the matter of Mr. Nunamaker's death. Do you understand, Mr. Reno?"

I didn't speak.

"If you continue to interfere, some very bad things could happen to you or your friends. Accidents, of course, but it would be sad for that lovely long legged stewardess to have such bad fortune. Would it not, Mr. Reno?"

I had heard enough. "Listen, you overstuffed illegal immigrant," I shouted. "If I even THINK something might happen to her or one of my friends, I'll separate your ugly head from that gold necklace and send it to your drug crazy family in a box! Do YOU understand, Mr. Escobar?" I was loud, and he realized he had finally been successful in pissing me off.

"My, my," he said calmly while refreshing his drink. "My associates said you had a bad mouth, it seems they were right."

"It isn't my mouth you need to be concerned about," I continued to shout. "I don't like your threats, I don't like your associates, I don't like your methods and I especially don't like YOU. So, if this meeting is over, I've got other things to do." I was reaching for the door.

"Not yet," he said motioning to the door. "I'm not making threats, Mr. Reno. These documents are very important to me and are worth an enormous amount of money. So these aren't threats, they are promises. If you find this animal doctor before my associates, will you be willing to retrieve those documents and give them to me?"

"Never," I said.

"I thought so," he replied as he reached over his left shoulder and pressed a button mounted on the wall. The doors unlocked.

The door to my right opened, I quickly exited the limo and stepped back on the garage floor. Then somebody turned out the lights.

~

Opening my eyes, I saw Joe fanning me with a newspaper and felt Marcie wiping my face with a damp cloth. I could hear voices, but the words made no sense. Evidently, I was lying on my office couch and had somehow been rescued.

Speaking was difficult and each word hurt as it came out of my mouth. "What happened?" I managed to utter.

"Joe went looking for you and found you in the parking garage," Marcie said. "Apparently, he scared away whoever hit you, because he saw two guys in a black car drive away in a hurry. Can you tell us what happened?"

"I'm not sure," I said. "But I think I had a disagreement with a Columbia drug lord."

"What?" Joe yelled.

"Never mind, I'll tell you about it later. Aren't you supposed to be on your way to Humboldt?" I asked Joe.

"Yes, but I came back in to ask you to call Leroy Epsee and tell him I would be stopping by this afternoon. When I couldn't find you, I went looking. It's a good thing I did."

"A very good thing indeed. You go ahead and hit the road; I'll call Leroy's office and tell them you will be stopping by to introduce yourself. For now, I'm going to take a couple of aspirin and sit here until this head throb goes away."

"Okay, I'm leaving, Marcie," Joe said to her. "You stay with him until it's safe for him to walk and drive."

"Don't worry, I'll take care of him," Marcie said.

Back to Humboldt

 It took me over two hours before I felt ready to point the Ford toward Humboldt. I know Liz had mentioned a party and I sure hoped it wasn't tonight; I wasn't up to it.

The sun had already said 'goodnight' when I finally parked the Ford in front of Cabin 4 at Chiefs. Joe's car was parked out front of Chiefs and we had some serious catching up to do.

He was dancing with Barbie when I walked in!

I found a stool and Nickie found me a Jack and Coke. She pointed at the dancing couple and said, "Ain't they cute?"

"As a 'butter bean', my mother always said! I take it you've already met Joe. Have you spoiled him already?"

"Absolutely. Can I take him home tonight?" she said laughing.

"Help yourself. But I need him tomorrow, so let's hope Ronnie or Barbie don't disagree with the arrangement!"

"They better not. Besides, I've had enough of Ronnie today; he has been out of control since breakfast," Nickie snapped.

"Oh yeah?" I asked. "Anything new?"

"New, old, used – he doesn't care. If they looked like a woman, he's been chasing them all day. Maybe if I bring home a new puppy, he'll act better."

"Nickie, Joe's not a puppy. I know he can bite, I've seen him!"

"Well, he's cute as a puppy. Maybe Barbie will want to take him home," she laughed.

"Whatever. But call your waitress off; I need to spend some time with Joe. Has he eaten?" I asked.

"No, said he was waiting on you. Steaks good?"

"Perfect. Now call off Barbie, and I'll be outside on the phone. Tell Joe to get a drink and comfortable at the bar so we can talk. Have we got rooms already?" I asked.

"He's in 3 and you have your usual 4. I'll get Ronnie working on the steaks."

From the outside payphone I called Leroy to see if anything new had developed, it hadn't. He had spent an hour with Joe and complimented me on my choice; Joe had made a good impression with Leroy and his two deputies, and that was good. I told him we should plan on lunch tomorrow; I needed to brief him on a few things. Leroy agreed.

Reluctantly, I called Liz next. She answered on the first ring.

"Hey handsome," she said. "Glad you could make it. What time you coming over?"

"Liz, I need a rain check. Today started off great and then went downhill in a hurry. I'm afraid I wouldn't be good company. You said Mary Ellen was having a party, is that tomorrow night?"

"No, it's tomorrow afternoon – 4:00 PM at the Country Club. You are coming, right?" I could almost see her face when she asked that.

"Yes, I will be there at 4:00 PM promptly." I hoped.

"Okay, since you're no fun tonight, Mary Ellen and I are meeting Judy, Gerald and Jack at the club for drinks. If you change your mind, you know where to find us."

"Go have fun," I offered. "Joe and I have some work to do tonight, I'll see you tomorrow."

When I walked back in, Joe had successfully separated himself from Barbie and found a stool next to mine. We spent the next couple of hours having dinner, discussing my meeting with Julio Escobar and planning strategy for our next move.

I needed Joe to work on the Harry and Linda Smiley situation. It was my theory that our two Mafia friends had loaded her up with money and suggested she disappear for a few days, but I wasn't sure why. If they had run down and killed her husband, Harry Smiley, it was for a reason. And that reason probably had something to do with the disappearance of Dr. Jack Preston and/or the missing papers Julio Escobar needed. My guess was Harry had stolen the papers, and he was killed because they believed he still had them. When that didn't work, they went hunting for Dr. Preston. What I couldn't figure was them paying Linda Smiley to leave town, unless they figured she knew more than she should and too many bodies lying around would make things more complicated. Or maybe she was dead already, and it was just supposed to look like she left town. In that case, her 'payoff' was a permanent one!

I was going to take Billy Grayton's suggestion and talk with his jockey, Miguel Rivera. It was probably a dead end or information I already had, but it needed to be done.

Joe and I would meet Leroy at the Ramble Inn for lunch tomorrow, and then my afternoon would be spent sipping wine and collecting donations for Mary Ellen's latest fundraiser. Fun would be had by all!

I called it an early night. Joe stayed to entertain Barbie and Nickie!

~

Joe and I enjoyed Ronnie's breakfast special and then headed off in our separate directions. He was going to start with another visit to the Smiley residence; mine started with another visit to *'Sugar Creek Farms'*.

Billy was on his tractor as I pulled into his long driveway. I stopped and he pulled over to the fence where I was parked.

"Hi, Carson, anything new?" he asked.

"Some, but the clues are hard to find and mostly misleading. I've taken your suggestion and stopped to talk with your jockey, Miguel Rivera. Is he around?"

"Yes, he's working out one of our horses. You'll find him somewhere around the training track or at the barn. Do you need me?" he asked.

"Not now. I'll let you know before I leave." I got back in the Ford and headed up the hill to the main house and training track.

Miguel was working a beautiful black stallion, and he was in full stride when I pulled up and parked. Evidently, he was expecting me, because he soon brought the horse to a walk and then turned him over to a stable hand for cooling down.

Miguel quickly came out of the track gate and walked over to where I had parked. He was short, as are most jockeys, but stout. He introduced himself, shook my hand and suggested we go inside the stable to talk.

"Miguel, thanks for talking with me; Billy had suggested that I do so. Is there anything you can add to the mysterious events that happened at *'Nunamaker Stables'*?" I asked as we took seats around a small table.

"First, I want you to know that Todd Randal did not kill Mr. Nunamker," he said frankly.

"Okay, I accept that," I said. "But if he didn't, who did?"

"Probably those Mafia people that he owed all the money to, maybe, but I do not know."

"Okay, but there are some problems with that theory, are there any other suspects you can think of?" I asked.

"No, none," he replied shaking his head.

"Okay, I have just two other questions, and then I'll let you get back to your work. Why is Todd Randal lying about his relationship with Mrs. Nunamaker?"

"I don't know. You'll need to ask him that question," he said without blinking.

"Okay, second question. Where does Dr. Jack Preston fit into this whole mess?"

"You want me to guess?" he asked with a frown.

"Sure, I'll take guesses. What do you think?"

"I think Aaron Nunamaker was making him add false certifications to the Jockey Club on a lot of his stock. I think Nunamaker was using his real stock to pay those Mafia guys for his debts, and Dr. Preston sobered up one day and got tired of it. That's what I think," he answered frankly.

"Do you think Dr. Preston could have killed him?" I asked.

"Possible, but I doubt it. You'll need to ask him that question."

"I will, when I find him. Miguel, thanks for your information; you've been a big help." He hadn't.

I left and waved at Billy, as I made my way down the highway and back to the main road.

~

Leroy and Joe were already at the Ramble Inn when I arrived. Unlike most days, it wasn't crowded and we had no trouble finding a suitable table to eat and talk.

Ramble Inn

I stopped at the counter to order a burger and fries before joining Joe and Leroy.

"You guys eating healthy today?" I asked them both.

"Carson," Leroy replied, "it isn't possible to eat healthy at the Ramble Inn. You know that."

"I thought hamburger was one of the 5 food groups. Have I been misled?" I laughed.

"You are living proof that hamburgers are required to sustain life," Leroy laughed. "But let's talk about something more serious. Joe has filled me in about your encounter with Julio Escobar and his two muscle men. Do we need to be concerned with their threats?"

"Leroy, I'm not sure, but something is really troubling me. Let's assume that our suspicions are correct, and the Mafia has taken some very valuable horses from *Nunamaker Stables'* in payment for gambling debts. And let's assume that Dr. Preston has some important papers that belong to Julio Escobar. Escobar did, in fact, tell me that, but it makes no sense that he would be concerned about the thoroughbred Jockey Club certifications. First, he is taking the horses to Columbia for sale, racing or stud, and I'm not sure these certifications mean much in South America. Second, if they did, he would just have them forged. I suspect that is what Dr. Preston had been doing for other horses at *Nunamaker Stables'* anyway, so why go to all the trouble?" I said.

"Okay, if it's not the thoroughbred certifications, then what does Dr. Preston have that Escobar needs?" Joe asked.

"I think when the doctor took the thoroughbred papers; he also took the medical records for the horses. Those would include health and wellness, injuries, treatments and most importantly vaccination records. I think Escobar has these horses somewhere, but is having trouble getting clearance to ship them out of the country. I think these horses are sitting in some equestrian warehouse, being held by US Customs waiting on proper medical clearance. Clearance he can't get without those documents Dr. Preston stole."

"Carson, you've had some wild theories in the past, but now you might have surpassed your previous efforts," Leroy said.

"Leroy, think about it," I said. "He wants these horses for himself. Besides, he couldn't sell them in the US anyway, and getting them quickly out of the country makes sense. We know Escobar needs something from Dr. Preston, and I'm betting it has nothing to do with Jockey Club certification. Harry Smiley got himself killed because he probably assisted Dr. Preston in stealing the documents. The bad guys went after him when they couldn't find Dr. Preston, but evidently Harry had already gotten rid of them. Next, they go to his wife, Linda, and give her some money to go away. But she fooled them, and left that house full of kids behind with her sister. The bad guys will search that house, if they haven't already. So, if anybody needs protection, it is probably those kids. What do you think?"

"I think I'm going to have someone from the County or State go and take custody of those kids," Leroy said quickly.

"Good idea. Now Joe, did you have any success looking for Linda Smiley?" I asked.

"None. I talked with her sister and it was mostly a waste of time. Their parents are dead and they have no other siblings. I talked with neighbors and no one has seen her. It seems she got into her car and drove off; however, they did believe it strange that she would just walk away and leave her kids."

"So do I," I added, "which makes me think she is probably dead. What kind of car does she drive? Did you find out?"

"A 59 Volkswagon – dark blue."

"Leroy, I think it might be a good idea to get an APB out on her car. I also suggest you have Jeff and Scotty give that house a good search, when you get the sister and kids out. I doubt that anything is there, but we know the bad guys will search it, maybe we should do it first."

"Okay Carson," Leroy said. "You're giving me a lot of work, but you're not giving me any reason to believe Todd Randal didn't kill Aaron Nunamaker."

"I know, but this is all tied together - somehow. Jack Logan has got a preliminary hearing scheduled for Todd next week, and I've got to give him some ammunition. Joe and I are going to work on some strategy to do that."

Leroy got up and said, "You guys share my burger. I've got to find somebody to take care of those kids. You've got my attention."

Leroy left Joe and me to finish our lunch and do some planning.

"Joe, I've got some difficult assignments for you. You ready?" I asked as we finished our burgers.

"I'm ready, boss. Just point me in the right direction."

"First, I need to know where our two Mafia friends are staying. James Henry Lewis and Johnie Gibson are bunking in some local motel, either close to Humboldt, in Humboldt or maybe Jackson. I think that information will come in handy."

"Okay. What else?" Joe asked.

"Second, I want you to secure the license plate numbers from the personal vehicles of everyone involved in this mess: Aaron and Susan Nunamaker - Billy and Amanda Grayton- Eddie Merrick, the Nunamaker jockey – Justin Avery, the Nunamaker trainer – Miguel Rivera, the Sugar Creek jockey and don't forget Todd Randal. I also need you to get the license numbers of all farm vehicles and trucks associated with '*Sugar Creek Farms*' and '*Nunamaker Stables*'."

"Okay, but why?" he asked.

"I have a hunch somebody in this group might have been taking some airplane flights we don't know about. Airport parking companies collect license numbers of all vehicles that use their lots. When you get the numbers, we're going to check your information with McKeller Field in Jackson and the Memphis Airport to see if any of our suspects have parked there recently."

"Okay. What else?" Joe asked.

"Here's the tough one. We need to find an equestrian shipment that is being held in US Customs. Since we don't know the port and we don't know the ship, it might be difficult. The ship's registry could be any country, not necessarily a South American one. The port could also be anywhere, but my first choices would be New Orleans and Houston. My next choices would be Fort Lauderdale and Miami – not every port would handle these types of shipments."

"That is a tough one," Joe added.

"I know. Go to the sheriff's office and have them set you up with an office and phone. Use your head and instinct, I can't guide you any further than that."

"Okay. What are your plans?" Joe asked.

"I need to have an interview with Susan Nunamaker, but the rest of my day is booked. I'll plan that for tomorrow. Meanwhile, this afternoon I'll be at the Humboldt Country Club at a fundraiser with Liz. You can reach me there if you need me. Just call the bar and have the bartender Nuddy find me."

We finished our lunch and I went back to Chiefs to freshen up and dress for this afternoon's event.

~

Mary Ellen Maxwell was a widow, a Humboldt socialite and the owner of Maxwell Trucking. She and Liz are best friends, and we met during a case that involved the murder of Mary Ellen's husband. Judy Strong works as executive vice president at Maxwell Trucking. She and Jack Logan met during the same case and have become very close friends. Gerald Wayne is the owner of Wayne Knitting, and he and Mary Ellen have recently become a pair in the Humboldt social circle.

Wayne Knitting

116

This afternoon's event was a social fundraising sponsored by Mary Ellen for the benefit of a local homeless shelter. All the Humboldt elite were there, invited to write their checks for another worthy cause. Carson Reno, Memphis private detective, was there as a guest of Elizabeth Teague and right in the middle of it.

I spent the first hour upstairs shaking hands with old friends, and eventually writing a generous check for Mary Ellen. Liz was bouncing from table to table and conversation to conversation, this gave me an opportunity to slip to the downstairs bar and visit with Nuddy, the bartender, and get a real drink.

Nathan Crouch was the owner of Humboldt's Cadillac dealership, the owner of a couple of dirt stock car tracks and the owner of some fine horses. He stopped at the bar while I was talking with Nuddy.

"Nathan," I said. "Good to see you. Have you left all your money upstairs with Mary Ellen?"

"Ha! Not yet but my wife is still there. It isn't over yet!" he laughed.

"Have you got some time to visit with me?" I asked.

"Not now, I need to get back upstairs and protect my check book! Stop by the track tonight," he suggested. "I'll be in Gadsden racing tonight, come see me there."

"Will do," I said as he headed back upstairs.

I had just ordered my second drink when Jack Logan took the stool next to mine.

"Carson, I've got a hearing next week! What have you got for me?" Jack asked.

"We're working on it, and I know you don't want to hear that. But we have a lot of people telling us a lot of lies. I'll have something for you before the hearing, promise. Has Todd changed his story yet?" I asked.

"Not really, and that's strange. He knows that I know he's lying, but he's protecting somebody. I'm not going to be able to do much unless you give me some ammunition for my hearing," he said shaking his head.

"We're working on it," I said again.

Eventually Liz, Judy, Mary Ellen and Gerald came and joined us in the downstairs bar. We found a table and had an uneventful evening over drinks, dinner and wine. Mary Ellen had raised a lot of money, so that part of the day had been successful.

~

Dinner was finished when Liz asked, "Okay, Carson, what are doing for the rest of the evening, dancing and a movie?"

"Liz, we're going to a stock car race. You ever done that?"

"No, and it's not going to start today! I have my limits, Mr. Reno, and that is outside of them. You find yourself some hotrod honey and forget me!" She was being difficult.

"Come on, Liz! You can stay in the car. I won't be long. Then we'll go to the VFW for some dancing. Okay?" Was I begging?

"You'll have my company for 15 minutes at this fiasco, and leave the car keys with me. If you take longer, I'll leave your ass with the rednecks," she was not kidding.

"Deal," I said nodding.

We left the group with a promise to do it again soon. Jack and I would talk tomorrow, Monday at the latest.

~

The Gadsden Speedway was a quarter-mile dirt track located 6 miles southwest of Humboldt on Highway 70/79.

Saturday night was race night, and the 'good old boys' brought out their stock cars for a fun night of racing, rubbing, wrecking and drinking.

In addition to owning the local Cadillac dealership, Nathan Crouch owned the speedway, and usually had a few of his own cars in the weekly show. Nathan was also a horse owner and had several thoroughbreds that were housed at '*Nunamaker Stables*' and had all been reportedly lost in the fire.

I left Liz in the car and made my way into the track. I found Nathan sitting in the announcer's booth watching the action and sipping on something out of a paper cup.

"Carson, my friend," he said as he stood up to greet me. "Good to see you, sit down and pull up a paper cup. I've got just the cure for whatever illness, ailment, lost love or woman problem you might have."

"I'm sure you do, Nathan." I never got the chance to refuse. He had already poured me a cup before I got seated.

"What drags you out with the rednecks?" he asked.

"Did you lose any horses in the '*Nunamaker Stable*' fire?"

"Sure did, son. Three of the finest thoroughbred race horses in West Tennessee and three of the fastest too. But you must have known that already, right?"

"I thought you did, but I wasn't sure. Would you be able to identify those horses?" I asked.

"Identify? Hell boy, they hardly had enough to bury, much less identify. Everything in that barn was cooked – and I mean WELL DONE," he laughed.

"What I mean is, could you identify those horses if they didn't die in the fire? Could you prove they were your horses?" I asked.

Nathan gave me a very funny look. "Hell boy," he said again. "You telling me my horses didn't burn in that fire? Is that what you are saying?"

"Bare with me a minute," I started. "Would you be able to provide conclusive proof and documentation that they are your horses? Providing they are alive?"

"Carson, supposedly all the official records burned with the animals or that drunk veterinarian lost them, but I'm no idiot. I never trusted that drunk, and about 6 months ago I had a vet from Memphis do another certification. Those records are at home in my safe. Is that what you want to know?"

"Nathan, that's EXACTLY what I wanted to know - thank you! Now, if you'll forget we ever had this conversation, I'll forget to tell Leroy about this shit that you tried to get me to drink! Is this the same stuff you're using for fuel in those race cars?" I laughed.

"Ha! No, but now that you bring it up, it might not be a bad idea."

"Well, I would suggest you don't smoke for a couple of hours after you drink it, if you know what I mean."

"Carson, I do know what you mean," he laughed. "Now, if you find my horses I want to be the first one to know. Okay?"

"That's a deal, but don't mention this conversation to anyone until we talk again," I said as I got up to leave.

"I won't. And while you're leaving, watch that number 43 running down there. That's my car, and it's been kicking ass for the last year."

When I got back to the car it was EMPTY! Liz was not where she was supposed to be – sitting in the car.

She had given me 15 minutes and I only used 10, something was wrong. As I'm deciding what to do, I hear her distinctive laugh. It was coming from an area next to the track fence, an area where spectators would watch from their car, or from the bed of their truck.

I walked over to the fence, and there she was. Sitting on the tailgate of a pickup truck, swinging her legs and talking to a woman I didn't recognize.

"Carson, I want you to meet someone," she said cheerfully. "This is my friend Tammy. Her husband is driving the number 12 racecar; it's red with white letters. Did you see it?"

"I'm afraid I didn't. Did it win?" I asked them both.

"No silly, it crashed. I can't believe you missed it. It was exciting and nobody got hurt. Isn't that nice?" Liz was actually giddy over the whole thing.

"How do you know Tammy? Did you girls go to school together?" I asked stupidly.

"Well, no – I don't think so. We just met a few minutes ago. Tammy did we go to school together?" she asked the woman.

At this point, I believe Tammy thinks Liz is crazy and I'm ready to agree with her. They continued to chat about cars, kids and subjects I'm not familiar with, and it was like they had known each other since birth! I stood back and watched the races; it had been a while since I had been dirt track racing.

Eventually their conversation ended and Liz dragged me back to the car.

"That was fun," she said. "We should do it again sometime."

I said nothing and pointed the car toward the VFW. Someday I'll try harder to understand women. For now I just accept whatever happens.

~

It was Saturday night and the VFW was crowded. Some local group was providing the entertainment and actually they were pretty good.

We danced until the band quit, almost 1 o'clock, which was much too late. I had a full day tomorrow and she was headed back to Memphis to catch a flight to the West Coast.

Liz had eggs, so we stayed at her place.

Clues

I showered and changed in my cottage at Chiefs the next morning. Joe's car was not there, so I assumed he had already started working on his healthy task list.

I grabbed a coffee to go and pointed the Ford toward '*Nunamaker Stables*'. I was going to have my first interview with Susan Nunamaker. Dr. Jack Preston's office was on the way, so I decided to give it one last try. One of Leroy's police cruisers was parked out front, and I stopped to check it out.

The front door was open, and as I entered I could see the place was a mess. File cabinets open and turned over with papers strewn all over the floor. Jeff Cole was writing in his note pad.

"More trouble?" I asked.

"Second break-in over the past three days," Jeff said shaking his head. "Evidently they didn't find what they were looking for the first time because this time they really made a mess. We can't determine if anything is missing, but the medical supply cabinet seems to be untouched. They were looking for paper files and only Dr. Preston would be able to tell us if they found them."

"And still no luck finding him?" I asked.

"Nope. What brings you out here this morning?" Jeff asked.

"I'm headed to '*Nunamaker Stables*'," I answered as I carefully walked around the papers and equipment strewn across the floor. "I haven't interviewed Susan yet. I've put it off for obvious reasons, but it's time to get that done. Tell Leroy I'll stop by this afternoon and brief him on my conversations."

"Will do," Jeff added as he went back to taking notes.

"Jeff, did somebody go to the Smiley residence and take care of those kids?" I asked.

"Leroy had the local family services people out there yesterday afternoon. I understand they have relocated the kids to a foster home until the mother shows up. I accompanied their representative to the house, and that is one crazy place. The smell is overwhelming and that sister is crazy as a bat, she needs professional help. The woman just kept yelling about somebody coming to bring her money – we had to physically remove her!"

"Did you guys search the house?" I asked.

"Sure did. Found nothing, unless you consider dirty diapers nothing! Because there were plenty of them!" he laughed.

"Understand," I said. "I'm headed to '*Nunamaker Stables*'. Talk with you later."

~

My second visit to '*Nunamaker Stables*' was quite different from the first. This is a giant property and it seemed much larger without all the police and emergency vehicles parked everywhere.

124

I drove directly through the large gate and up to the main house. Since I was unannounced and had no appointment, I wasn't sure what I might find.

A servant answered after my first knock and told me that Mrs. Nunamaker was having brunch on the patio. He escorted me through the house and to a large patio overlooking the practice track, several pastures and the barn area – including the burned stable.

Susan Nunamaker finally appeared and was a strikingly attractive woman. She was middle to late forty's, and had taken care of herself very well. Susan had medium length blonde hair, perfectly manicured nails and fresh makeup. However, it was apparent that Susan was under stress, and the makeup was having trouble covering an obvious lack of sleep.

I introduced myself. "Susan, my name is Carson Reno and thank you for seeing me this morning. I am working with Leroy Epsee to help resolve the issue of your husband's murder. Do you have time to talk?"

"I thought they had the man that murdered Aaron? Haven't they arrested Todd Randal?" she said with somewhat of a sneer.

"Yes, he has been arrested, but we want to make sure Todd is the person responsible. That is the proper thing to do for everyone concerned," I was trying to soft sell my being there.

"Mr. Reno, I know you are working for the attorney who is defending Todd. So don't bullshit me. Okay?"

She poured herself a cup of coffee and motioned for the servant to bring another cup for me.

"Start with your questions and let's get this over. I have a hair appointment in an hour, so you don't have long," she said with a matter of fact tone.

"All right, I can do that. I'll skip the normal police type questions, you're already answered those, but I do have some they might have overlooked. First, what is your relationship with Todd Randal?"

"What do you mean by relationship?" she snapped.

"I mean relationship. Friends, enemies, good friends, close friends, not close friends — how would you describe you and Todd Randal?" I asked.

"Friends, I guess you could say we were good friends, not close, but good friends. Is that what you mean?"

"Yes it is. I've been told by some of your employees that Todd spent a lot of time here at your house. How do you explain that?"

"I explain it as friends, just like I said. Besides, we had a lot of business dealings together. We ARE both in the horse business — didn't you know that?" she was being defensive.

"Okay, I'll leave it at that. Can you tell me why your husband was having business dealings with the Memphis Mafia and some other known criminals from South America?"

She sat upright in her chair and took a sip of coffee. "I don't know a lot about my husband's business, outside of our racing operations and breeding services. You might check with our trainer, Justin Avery, but I doubt he will have much to add."

"I intend to do that. What kind of business would you and Todd Randal discuss, when he was here discussing business?" I was really touching some nerves – it showed.

"Horse business, Mr. Reno. I thought we had already covered that," she snapped again.

"I understand you were in Hallandale Beach, Florida at a race when your husband was murdered. Do you normally accompany your horses to these types of events?"

"Sometimes, but this was special. We were running a new mare in the claiming race and I wanted to be there. Is something wrong with that?"

"I wasn't suggesting that there was. But you and Mr. Avery drove to Florida, is that right?"

"That is the only way to get a horse to a race track that I am aware of." She was not making this easy.

"But couldn't he have driven and you flown down for the race?" I asked.

"Perhaps, but I didn't. Do you have more questions?"

"Just one. Who do you think killed your husband and why?"

"Todd Randal and I have no idea why – ask him! They never liked each other, maybe they fought, how would I know?" She was almost shouting.

"Why didn't they like each other?" I tried.

"You said a few questions and now you turn this into an interrogation. I have to go get ready for my appointment. Thank you for visiting my home. I hope you come back again under better circumstances."

Susan Nunamaker got up and walked back into the house, leaving me with her unfinished brunch and a still empty coffee cup!

I found my way out of the house without assistance, and drove back up to the burned barn. My hopes were to find Justin Avery and have that interview. One of the workers told me that Justin Avery was not there and was, in fact, out of town – they didn't know where.

~

My drive back to town found the 59 black Chevrolet Impala on my tail again. They followed until I turned into Chiefs, where Leroy's cruiser and Joe's car were parked. I guess their interest in me went sour, because they continued south on 22nd.

Both Joe and Leroy were sitting at the counter having lunch. I joined them and ordered my usual – a hamburger.

"Okay, Joe, you first. What have your detective skills uncovered?" I asked with a laugh.

"Not much boss, but I do know where those two bad guys are staying. They are rooming at the Tyler Towers Motel on 22nd Avenue.

Tyler Towers Motel

"Okay, that's good information. It might come in handy," I said.

Leroy looked at me. "And why might it come in handy? Are you planning on taking these guys on?"

"It just might come in handy, leave it at that," I said bluntly before turning on my barstool and looking at Joe. "Joe, you got anything on an equestrian shipment being held by customs?" I asked.

"Not yet, but I have a lot of calls that haven't been returned. Leroy has set me up in a vacant office and I've got use of a phone. His deputies volunteered to take return calls if they come in when I'm not there. I've also gathered all the license plate numbers you asked for, but I haven't gotten them to the airport parking businesses yet."

"License numbers?" Leroy shouted. "Carson, what kind of crazy scheme are you after now? You're working my department overtime already, and I have absolutely NOTHING to show for it!"

"Calm down, Leroy. It's just a hunch. And if it works out, we'll know a lot more truth about this situation than we know now. If it doesn't, then we'll try something else. I've got to get Jack Logan something for his preliminary hearing, and I'm running out of time and options."

Nickie delivered my hamburger, then stood with her hands on her hips shaking her head at Leroy, Joe and me. "You boys act nice," she said walking away.

"Carson, I know you are trying to find reasons why Todd didn't kill Aaron Nunamaker," Leroy pleaded. "But, at some point you might just need to accept the fact that he did it."

"Leroy, I am NOT trying to find reasons why he didn't do it. I'm trying to get to the truth, and so far I can't find anybody willing to TELL the truth. It seems everybody is lying, but they are lying for different reasons. That's what I need to find out."

"I understand," Leroy shrugged. "I'm not picking on you; guess I'm as frustrated as you are."

"Do you have any idea where the trainer, Justin Avery, is?" I asked Leroy.

"No. Why?"

"Because he isn't at '*Nunamaker Stables*', and one of the workers told me he was out of town. Wouldn't you have instructed him to not leave town? Or, at least, not leave unless he told your office where he was going?" I asked.

"Justin Avery, and everybody else involved in this case, has explicit instructions not to leave town, you know that. And if he has left without telling my office, I'll arrest him when he does come back. I'll have Jeff or Scotty check on him this afternoon," Leroy said shaking his head.

"Please do, because I need to talk with him," I said. "Justin Avery is Susan Nunamaker's alibi, and unless he's different from everybody else, he's lying too!"

"Has Jack had any luck getting Todd to change his story?" Leroy asked us both.

"No, and that makes no sense either," I continued. "His story is that he drove back to Humboldt from Hot Springs after the Friday races. But we know he didn't, and spent that Friday night in Hot Springs registered at his hotel as Mr. and Mrs. Todd Randal. Now, unless a Mrs. Todd Randal suddenly shows up, we know he was with some unknown woman. I can assume his lying is to protect that unknown woman, but it just makes him look guiltier."

"Who do you think that woman was?" Joe asked looking at both of us.

"I don't know, and I'm sure Leroy doesn't either," I answered glancing at Leroy. "But if my hunch is right, we'll know a lot more when we get a report on those license numbers from the airport parking lots."

"Is that your way of telling me I need to get off this barstool and get busy?" Joe laughed.

"See Joe, that's one thing I like about you – you catch on quick!"

"I need to go too," Leroy said. "I'm going to check on the whereabouts of Mr. Justin Avery, and I'll let you know what I found out."

When Joe and Leroy left, Nickie walked over.

"You look frustrated, Mr. Reno. Would Mr. Jack Daniels be of any help?" she asked with a laugh.

"Nickie, you missed your calling. You should have been a mind reader. You are good at it, you know?"

"Practice, Mr. Reno, I've had plenty of practice. One Jack and Coke coming up!" she cheerfully said as she poured my drink.

Nickie was right, I was frustrated. With the exception of Dr. Preston and this unknown woman, I think we have all the pieces. I just needed to figure out how to put them together. Joe and I were going to work on finding Dr. Preston, I intended to find him one way or another – dead or alive. But this unknown woman was really bothering me. Who could it be? The logical answer is Susan Nunamaker, but something was wrong with that. If it were Susan, why would Todd try to protect her? With Aaron Nunamaker dead, what was the point? An affair between Todd and Susan would certainly put more suspicion on Todd and maybe even give him another motive for murder. But, it could also give some credibility to self-defense, if he wanted to try that path. However, I don't believe it was self-defense, because I don't believe he killed Aaron Nunamaker. Billy Grayton's words just kept coming back – *'he might have killed Aaron Nunamaker, but he could never have killed those horses'*. At this point, that's the only thing about this case that seemed to make any sense! But, Joe and I are going to work on fixing that, starting this afternoon.

~

Nickie has just refreshed my drink when Joe walked back in Chiefs. He took the stool next to me, looked at me and smiled.

"Okay," I said. "We all know you're cute, but what are you smiling about?"

"I found the horses. They are being held on a ship called 'South America Seas' in the port of New Orleans. Customs has prevented sailing until proper medical papers can be produced for fifteen horses scheduled for shipment and delivery to Columbia. The owner of the horses is listed as Julio Escobar with an address in Bogota, Columbia. This guy must have balls bigger than a basketball – he uses his real name!" Joe was excited.

"Sure he uses his real name, and why not?" I added. "These idiots don't fear anyone, and believe their muscle can fix any problem; however, it seems this time Dr. Jack Preston has gotten the better of everybody."

Nickie sensed the excitement and couldn't wait to join. "Now I have two handsome private detectives sitting at my bar, and they are both much happier than they were an hour ago. I would like to think I had something to do with the happiness, and know that I probably didn't, but you could lie and make me feel better!" she said laughing.

"Yes, you did," I added. "Please get this young man to my left a drink. I assure you he is old enough and I definitely know he has earned it!"

"Another Jack and Coke coming up," she said walking away.

"Joe, how did she know that was what you drink?" I asked.

"Beats me, guess she wants me to be just like you!" he laughed.

"I'm not sure I want that, but let's get back to business. When you finish that drink, I want you to go find Leroy. If he's not in his office, have Jeff or Scotty call him on his radio. I need Leroy to call U. S. Customs in New Orleans and tell them that those horses are stolen. He should tell them that some of the horses belong to a Mr. Nathan Crouch and we have documented proof of ownership. I'll contact Nathan and have him provide the documents to Leroy. Leroy and U. S. Customs can work out the details, but I want those horses on a truck and headed back here as quickly as possible. I'm pretty sure Nathan will be willing to pay for the truck. I'll go ask him."

"Okay, what else?" Joe asked.

"What else? You want more? Tell you what; I'm going to see Nathan Crouch while you're at the Sheriff's office. You meet me back here at five o'clock; we're going to visit a local bar I heard about."

"Huh?" he said with a frown.

"Never mind. Just be here at five o'clock. Did you get anything from the parking garages yet?"

"No, and it will be tomorrow before I hear anything. I had to get one of Leroy's deputies to use some muscle, the parking garage management wasn't very accommodating with my requests."

"Okay, well our use of his deputies might have irritated Leroy a little, but at least we'll get our information," I added.

"Hey, Carson," Joe asked as he was leaving. "What do you think these Mafia guys will do when they find out about us trying to get those horses?"

"Be really pissed, and I'm counting on that," I laughed.

Crouch Motor Company

I was hoping to get lucky and catch Nathan at his Cadillac dealership - I needed some luck. Fortunately, he was in his office and waved me back when he saw me walk in.

"Carson, it's great to see you again. You come by to trade cars or get another shot of that 'joy juice' I gave you at the track?" he said laughing.

"Neither," I said walking into his office. "I came to tell you I found your horses."

Nathan stood up and shouted, "You're kidding me – right?"

"No, I'm not kidding. You do want them back, don't you?"

"Absolutely. Forget the insurance, I want my horses," he was almost yelling.

"Then I need you to get your documentation and take it down to the sheriff's office now, no delays. Your horses are loaded on a ship docked in the port of New Orleans. And if the bad guys get their clearance before Leroy proves they are stolen; then they are headed to South American and gone forever."

"I'm leaving now," he said as he headed for the door.

"Nathan, one more thing," I yelled. "Can you spring for a truck to bring your horses and several others back to Humboldt?"

Nathan was standing in the doorway and pointed his finger at me. "Carson, I'll go down and ride them back if I have to!"

The 'DoLittle Inn'

 *J*oe was late getting back to Chiefs. Leroy was having difficulty with U. S. Customs, and they were definitely not going to release the horses without some documentation. Nathan finally showed up at the sheriff's office with his paperwork, and then he got on the phone. Nathan told the customs officers that he would be on the first plane to New Orleans, and would PERSONALLY be bringing those horses back to Humboldt. It was a done deal.

Joe and I jumped in the Ford and headed to Medina. He asked twice where we were headed before I finally broke down and told him - the '*DoLittle Inn*'.

'Oh shit' was his only comment.

The parking lot was almost full – cars, pickup trucks, and motorcycles were everywhere. Even an 18-wheeler was parked along the highway. It was a busy night at the *'DoLittle Inn'*.

I backed the Ford into an open area almost directly in front of the door, that gave us a clear path back to the highway for a hasty retreat. I put it in neutral and left the motor running.

"Joe," I said seriously. "Right or wrong, my approach has always been to meet these things head on. Gaining the advantage always allows the situation to play the way that I want it to, not the way someone else does. This might get rough, and I don't want you to get hurt, so bring your gun. If it becomes necessary to use it - you'll know when that time comes. Don't hesitate. When we walk in the door, I want you to quickly move to the left and find a seat, if you can. Watch my back. I'm leaving the motor running in the Ford because I don't intend to be in there very long, and I have a hunch we'll be leaving in a hurry. Okay?"

"Yes Carson, I'm ready... I think!" He seemed nervous.

"You'll do fine," I encouraged, "and one other thing. If for some reason I don't make it back out the door, I want you to get in this Ford and head straight to the sheriff's office. You have Leroy, Scotty, Jeff or somebody come drag my carcass out of this bar. Mother and Dad deserve to have a body to bury – I owe them that."

"Now you're scaring me, Carson. Don't do that." Joe's eyes were as big as saucers.

"Don't be scared and don't loose your cool. Shoot if you need to and run when appropriate, but don't let them know you're scared. Are you ready?" I asked.

"Let's do it," Joe said with some faint confidence.

Joe followed as we walked slowly up to the door. I was hoping we didn't greet some patron leaving early – we got lucky.

I pushed open the door of the *'DoLittle Inn'* and never missed a step walking to the back of the bar. Everyone turned and watched me, giving Joe a chance to enter unnoticed – I hoped.

I found the biggest and ugliest fellow in that area of the bar and walked up behind him. "Hey asshole," I said loud enough for everyone to hear. "I'm looking for Dr. Jack Preston. Do you know where I can find him?"

He turned around, looked down at me and said, "Go to hell," as he swung his huge right hand at my face. Luckily, this was just what I had expected.

I ducked, and then came up swinging my .38 – catching him squarely on his big jaw with the top of the gun. I could hear his teeth shatter, as he tumbled backwards over an empty table and onto the floor at the end of the bar.

As he fell, I heard the familiar sound of a beer bottle breaking somewhere behind me and to my right. I turned and pointed the .38 in my right hand with an outstretched arm. When I did, the tip of the barrel was almost touching the nose of, a somewhat, smaller fellow. He was holding a broken beer bottle in his right hand and had stopped in mid-step. His eyes were almost crossed, both looking directly down the barrel of my gun.

"Well, well – look what we have here," I said loudly to everyone in the bar. "This fellow has brought a beer bottle to a gun fight!"

Over his shoulder I could see Joe with his weapon drawn and in a semi crouched stance. He was holding his gun with both hands and swinging it from side to side, letting everyone know it would not be a good idea to make any quick moves.

My .38 was pointing directly at this little guy's nose and he was intensely focused on the business end of the gun – not moving a muscle.

I cocked it!

"Whoa, whoa, whoa," he said as he dropped the bottle. "We're not looking for trouble mister!"

"Oh, really? What were you planing to do with that beer bottle?" I asked calmly.

"Look mister. Put the gun away and we'll forgive and forget. OK?"

"No, it's not okay. I'm looking for Dr. Jack Preston and somebody in this bar is going to tell me where to find him. I don't want to shoot everybody, but I will until somebody tells me what I want to know. So I'll start with you, shorty," I said to the little guy. "Tell me where he is, or I'll move on to the next person."

"He's not…he's not here," the little guy stuttered.

"I know he's not here stupid. I asked where I could find him. You got 30 seconds." Joe still had the room covered, and I had bought some time. But I knew this bluff wasn't going to last forever.

"Ok, Ok. All I know is he's got a daughter that lives in Savannah and Jack goes there sometimes when he needs to hide. That's all I know mister. I don't know her name or address just that she lives in Savannah. OK?" The little guy was really nervous.

"Thank you, you have been a great help. Now, I need everyone to back up against that far wall – please move slowly," I said in a loud and calm voice. They began backing toward the wall, not turning their backs on either Joe or me. Oddly, they all had their hands up like we were robbing the place!

"My partner and I are going to be leaving now, and let you guys get back to your 'support group' meeting! But we will shoot the first bastard that walks out that door behind us – so give it some thought before you decide to follow us or go home early. And tell that big fellow lying over in the corner that I know a good dentist who can probably fix most of his teeth. Have him call me if he needs a recommendation."

Joe and I backed out the door – him first and then me. I slammed the door to get attention and then we both made our run for the Ford.

Looking back through the dust I made leaving the parking lot, I didn't see anyone open the door. That was good.

"Wow," Joe stammered when we finally hit the highway and cleared danger.

"Yes, wow!" I answered.

"Carson, what if those guys come after us? You left some pissed off people back there, not to mention the one who needs some major dental work."

"I don't think they will, or I don't think they'll come after us. My guess is they think the two bad guys who just roughed up the place were working for the mob, and not a couple of private detectives from Memphis," I hoped.

"So they'll go after them?" Joe asked.

"I'm going to plant a seed with our local Mafia friends. My idea is to get them to make the same visit we just made; however, I expect the patrons of the *'DoLittle Inn'* will be better prepared for the next visit."

"I'd like to see that," Joe exclaimed.

"No you wouldn't. I'm afraid our welcome at the *'DoLittle Inn'* has been all used up. We'll need to find another watering hole!" I laughed.

"So, now we go to Savannah?" Joe asked.

"No. Now YOU go to Savannah and as quickly as you can. Find that daughter and find Dr. Jack Preston. Use whatever means necessary, but I want you to hold onto him. Then I want you to call Leroy to come get him. I want him in custody with police protection as quickly as we can make it happen. I'll brief Leroy and tell him to expect your call."

"Done. And by the way Carson, that was quite a show you put on back there."

"Yes, it was – wasn't it?" I said with a grin.

Strategy

*I*t was almost midnight before Joe hit the road to Savannah, and I finally called it a night, with a big day planned tomorrow. Jack Logan was due back in town around noon and I had a lot to get accomplished before he arrived. This was Monday, the preliminary hearing was scheduled for Tuesday and we weren't ready. Most of my day would be spent at the sheriff's office.

Sheriff's Office and Jail

I skipped Ronnie's breakfast special and settled for a coffee to go. Hopefully, Leroy would have some donuts at his office – he did.

"Leroy," I said as I helped myself to more coffee and a donut, "I'm going to set up in your conference room. I've got some calls to make, and hopefully we'll hear from Joe this morning. He's in Savannah looking for Dr. Preston."

"You found him?" Leroy seemed surprised.

"Not yet, but we have a good lead that he has a sister living there. Joe drove down last night to check it out. If he finds him, I'll need you or one of your deputies to go get him. Okay?"

"Should I ask where or HOW you obtained this information?" he frowned.

"No, you shouldn't, so don't. Just tell me you'll go get him when Joe calls."

"We'll go get him, don't worry about that. I want to talk to him as much as you and Jack do. What are your plans?" Leroy asked suspiciously.

"I've got two calls to make, both concerning Dr. Preston. Then I've got to get this parking lot information sorted out from the Memphis and Jackson airports. I have a hunch we're going to need it for the hearing tomorrow. Jack and I will have a strategy and planning meeting when he gets here, and hopefully you'll have Dr. Preston by that time. You want to join us?"

"I would like to," Leroy nodded, "but the DA might not like it. I'm first on his witness list tomorrow. Did you know that?"

"No, but that is what I would have suspected. Do you know who else, if anybody, he plans to call?" I wondered.

"Not a clue, but if I find out, I'll let you know." Leroy wanted to help, I was certain of that.

I settled into the conference room and made my first call. It was to the Tyler Towers Motel and I was hoping I would NOT reach the person I was calling. I got lucky.

The desk clerk answered my call and I had her ring the room of James Henry King and Johnie Gibson. She came back on the line telling me no one answered and asked if I would like to leave a message.

"Yes please, I would," I said in a pleasant tone. "My name is Dr. Jack Preston and I believe Mr. King and Mr. Gibson have been looking for me. I have some important documents they need and we haven't been able to get together. Please tell them that I will be available to meet with them today at 1 o'clock at the '*DoLittle Inn*' in Medina. That's 1 o'clock today at the '*DoLittle Inn*' in Medina – you got that?"

She responded that she had the information and would pass it along to Mr. King and Mr. Gibson. Without my asking, she added that they were currently having breakfast in the dining area and should be returning to their room shortly. She would give them the message then.

My next call was to the '*DoLittle Inn*'.

After the fifth ring a rough voice answered, "Yeah, what do you want?"

"I'm calling with a complaint," I said loudly.

"Oh, yeah? Well, call somebody who gives a shit!" He hung up.

I called back and he answered much quicker this time.

"Listen asshole," I shouted before he could speak. "Don't hang up, or I'll knock your teeth out like I did to that big idiot yesterday. Understand?"

He said nothing.

"I got some bad information yesterday, so I'm coming back today and we're going to try again. This time I'm leaving with the right information or no one's going to leave – standing up anyway. You pass the word around; I'll see you about noon." I hung up.

I told the bad guys one o'clock, figuring they wouldn't wait. I told the '*DoLittle Inn*' noon so they would be ready when the bad guys got there. I might let Leroy know about it later. He would need to go over and pick up the pieces, but I didn't want him there for the excitement.

~

Scotty Perry was manning the front desk and taking calls. I could see him from the conference room window and he was on the phone and waiving for me to join him.

He put his hand over the receiver and said, "This is the lady from the Memphis parking garage. She's got a match on a couple of your license numbers." Scotty handed me the phone.

I wrote down the information as she went through the list of license numbers with the dates they had used the parking garage. Part of the information was what I had suspected; the other part was hard to believe!

Back in the conference room, I made follow-up calls to the airlines confirming dates, times and destinations of our travelers. It was good information, but some of it was difficult to swallow.

Despite my disappointment, the plan was coming together. Joe called and he had already located Dr. Jack Preston. He had him in his car and was headed back toward Humboldt. Leroy would meet them both in Jackson and bring Dr. Preston straight to the jail.

The District Attorney for Gibson County was Griffin Hawks. I knew Griffin professionally, but not personally, although we had shared drinks and conversation at a few Humboldt social functions. I knew him to be a fine and capable lawyer with serious political aspirations, and a worthy adversary for my friend, Jack Logan.

Griffin entered the sheriff's office while I was on the phone with Joe. He waved at me through the window as Scotty escorted him upstairs for his interview with Todd Randal. I was also quite sure he would want to talk with Dr. Jack Preston, when Leroy got him back in town. Everyone was getting ready for the big day tomorrow.

My donut energy had expired and I needed some lunch. Jack wasn't due for an hour and neither was Joe or Leroy, so I headed back to Chiefs for lunch.

~

Ronnie's meatloaf special just didn't have the right 'ring' to it. I ordered my usual, a hamburger.

"Can I get you a Jack and Coke to go with that burger?" Nickie asked.

"Not yet, but hold that thought. I'm quite sure this afternoon you'll get a different answer."

"Oh, yeah? What's going on?" She was probing.

"Jack Logan and I are preparing for the hearing tomorrow. We'll both need some 'alcohol stimulation' later today, I'm sure. And speaking of 'stimulation' – where is that new waitress? Barbie?" I asked looking around the room.

"Don't ask," she said frowning.

"I just did," I exclaimed. "Did something happen?"

"Almost," she said while wiping the counter for the fifth time.

"Almost what?" I asked again. This was getting silly.

"Something almost happened," she said still wiping the counter.

"Look Nickie, this isn't an interrogation. Just tell me what happened so I don't have to pry for information."

"Okay Carson, I'll tell you. I had to fire Barbie. My carhop manager, Tommy Trubush, caught her and one of the carhops necking in the backseat of a car that was parked out back. You satisfied?" She was frustrated.

"No, I'm not satisfied. That doesn't sound like 'almost' to me. That sounds like a definite. What do you mean by 'almost'?" I asked again.

"Carson, I liked that girl, but my judgement was all wrong. I thought her little wiggles were good for business, and they probably were, but she was bad for everything else. Ronnie admitted that she had made a move on him, but he claims nothing happened. However, knowing what I know now, and knowing Ronnie – that wouldn't have been true for very long. I can handle him doing a lot of things, but making 'woopie' with the help is something I could not handle."

"Hell, Nickie, I thought there was something serious," I laughed. "You had me going for a minute. You seemed so upset."

"I am upset and it was serious!" she snapped. "I'm mad at myself. I know better."

"Don't beat yourself up. Just go find another waitress with a few less wiggles. It will all work out," I assured her.

"I know," she said. "Hey, where is that partner of yours, Joe? I haven't seen him since yesterday."

"My ASSOCIATE, Joe Richardson, is returning from Savannah. In fact, he should already be back. I better go see about him. Keep your chin up and keep smiling, Nickie. I'll see you this afternoon for that drink."

I hurriedly finished my burger and then headed the Ford back to the sheriff's office.

While I was at lunch, both Jack and Joe had made it to Humboldt and they were waiting on me in the conference room.

"Where's Dr. Preston?" I asked when I walked in.

"He's upstairs with the DA and Leroy," Joe answered. "But don't worry, he told me everything during our ride back to Jackson."

I pulled up one of the conference room chairs and got comfortable. "Okay, Mr. Associate Private Detective, please bring Jack and me up to date."

Joe spent the better part of the next hour telling us Dr. Preston's story. Most of it was what I had suspected, but he did add some interesting information concerning Justin Avery, the 'Nunamaker Stables' trainer. When Joe finished, I shared the information I had gotten from the parking garages and the airlines. Both Jack and Joe were surprised, but not shocked.

I sent Joe to check with Leroy on the whereabouts of Justin Avery and see if they had been able to locate him. I also needed him to check on Nathan Crouch and see if he had successfully made it to New Orleans and identified his horses. Then Jack and I shut the conference room door and spent the next two hours preparing for tomorrow's hearing. Joe was to meet us at Chiefs after 5 and we would all catch up then.

~

Joe was already at Chiefs and waiting in a corner booth when Jack and I walked in. It was 5:30.

"Carson," Joe asked, "where is Barbie?"

"Joe, don't ask," I ordered. "And especially, DON'T ask Nickie. I'll tell you all about it when we get back to Memphis. Okay?"

"Who's Barbie?" Jack asked.

"Don't ask," I said.

"Gee whiz," Jack exclaimed. "Seems like I must've missed something."

146

"You did!" Joe and I said together!

Nickie had just delivered our drinks when Leroy's cruiser pulled up out front. He walked in the door then straight to our table and sat down. He seemed irritated.

"Carson," he said glaring at me. "Do you know where I have been for the past two hours?"

"Talking to Dr. Jack Preston? Looking for Justin Avery?" I answered innocently.

"No," he said calmly. "Me and my deputies have been removing bodies, carrying for the wounded and arresting bad guys at a bar called the 'DoLittle Inn'. I think I heard you mention that place in a previous conversation. Didn't I?"

"Yes, you did, sheriff. And your advice was for me to stay away from there, right?" I nodded.

"That is correct. That is exactly what I told you," Leroy responded.

"And you know I always take your advice, right?" I was trying not to laugh.

"Bullshit Carson, you never take my advice!" Leroy was upset, but not angry. "And I don't know how you were responsible for what happened, but I know you were."

Joe is laughing and Jack has this 'I'm lost look' as he asks, "What is the 'DoLittle Inn'?"

"It's a place the sheriff told me to avoid, and I always do what the sheriff tells me to," I answered positively.

"Bullshit," Leroy said again.

"Tell us, Leroy. Exactly what did happen at the 'DoLittle Inn'?" I asked with a grin.

According to Leroy, two Memphis Mafia fellows had visited the bar yesterday and roughed up a couple of the local tough guys. He said they even knocked one of the guy's teeth out and then threatened to shoot everybody. Evidently, these two Memphis Mafia guys had not had enough, because they came back again today looking for more! Unfortunately for them, the local tough guys in the bar were ready this time. Why they came back and how the local guys in the bar knew they were coming, is still not clear.

Anyway, it seems that it all started when the Mafia guys pulled into the parking lot. One of the locals was waiting across the street in his 18-wheeler and smashed into the rear of the Mafia car, pushing it right through the front door of the *'DoLittle Inn'* – with them still in the car! That's when the gunfight started.

The Mafia guys were definitely overmatched, in both numbers and firepower, because they got shot up pretty good. Both will live, but probably spend several days, maybe weeks, in the hospital. Their car, a 59 Black Chevy, was a total loss. Between the 18-wheeler, the front of the bar and all the bullet holes, it had to be hauled off in pieces. There was one dead guy, a bar patron. Leroy wasn't sure if he died from gunfire or being run over by the car, but he had sustained injuries from both!

Four local tough guys were in the hospital and were also under arrest, along with the two Mafia fellows. But the *'DoLittle Inn'* was still in business; it seemed that not having a front wall on the bar made little difference.

We're laughing to tears, but Leroy is not finding the same humor we are.

"Carson, I don't know how you made that happen and please don't tell me. But one day you're going to get yourself into a situation that you can't talk or fight your way out of. And the Gibson County Sheriff's office might not be around to bail you out, just remember that," Leroy said frankly.

"You Protect and Serve. I always appreciate your assistance," I was still laughing.

When we were finally able to stop laughing, Jack asked, "Leroy, did you every find Justin Avery?"

"No, and now we have issued a warrant for his arrest. He's been subpoenaed to testify tomorrow, but we can't serve it until we find him."

"Did you learn anything interesting from Dr. Preston?" Jack asked Leroy.

"Yes, and you know I can't talk about that, so don't ask," he answered frankly.

"Leroy, can I buy you a drink and dinner?" I asked with a smile.

"You can buy me dinner, I'll skip the drink."

We had dinner and good conversation, avoiding discussions about tomorrow's hearing or what the District Attorney might have planned.

The hearing was scheduled to start at 9:00 tomorrow. We all made it a short evening and went to bed early.

Preliminary Hearing

A preliminary hearing is just that – preliminary. It has a two-fold purpose. First, to determine if a crime has been committed, and second, to determine if the accused is to be held over for trial. Both sides have the option of calling witnesses and presenting evidence, if they desire.

Gibson County Courthouse

Judge Graves called court to order at precisely 9:00 AM. Todd Randal was asked to stand before the court and enter a plea, his answer was 'Not Guilty'.

Judge Graves took his time in explaining the procedures of a preliminary hearing to the participants, the accused and the packed courtroom. Next, he asked District Attorney Griffin Hawks and Defense Attorney Jack Logan if they intended to present evidence and call witnesses. Both answered, "Yes."

"Very well," the judge replied. "Mr. Hawks, you may call your first witness."

As expected, Sheriff Leroy Epsee was called as the first witness. Leroy told the story as we had heard from him before. Jack objected as 'hearsay' when Leroy started to relate his conversation with jockey Eddie Merrick. Judge Graves sustained the objection.

The burned rifle was introduced as evidence, and Leroy testified how he verified Todd Randal as the owner of the rifle. Leroy then followed with testimony regarding his official questioning of Todd Randal, including his initial story and then how he had changed his story. Following that, Griffin Hawks turned the witness over to Jack Logan.

"Sheriff Epsee," Jack began. "Did you check the weapon for fingerprints?"

"We tried, but the heat from the fire had removed all fingerprints. What I mean is, we checked it for fingerprints and found none," Leroy replied.

"So sheriff, since you found no fingerprints, you assumed that the fire destroyed them. Is that correct?"

"What I am saying," Leroy repeated, "is that we found no fingerprints on the weapon. They could have been wiped off or the fire could have destroyed them. I have no way of knowing which."

"For the record, Sheriff Epsee, your testimony is that there were no fingerprints on the weapon, and you have no idea how they were removed. Is that correct?" Jack asked.

"Yes, that is correct," Leroy sighed.

"Okay. You testified that you identified the ownership of the weapon because Todd Randal's name was engraved on the rifle. Is that correct?" Jack asked.

"Yes, that is correct. And if you examine the rifle submitted into evidence, you can clearly see the name Todd Randal engraved into the barrel."

"Thank you, sheriff. And would you please confine your answers to just the question I ask? If I am looking for further clarification, I will make that clear." Jack was purposely irritating Leroy and it was working.

"Yes," Leroy answered with a sneer.

"Now, sheriff, when you asked Todd Randal about the rifle, how did he respond? What I mean is, where did he tell you he kept it, and when was the last time he saw it?"

"He claimed it was kept behind the seat of his truck, and he claimed he had not seen or used the weapon in several weeks."

"Okay," Jack was pacing back and forth while talking. "Did he also not tell you that his truck always remained unlocked, and it would have been easy for anyone to have removed the rifle without his knowledge?"

"Yes. But based upon..."

Jack interrupted Leroy. "I didn't ask for an opinion. I just asked for what Todd told you. Thank you for your answer. Now sheriff, how did you determine that this burned rifle was, in fact, the murder weapon?"

"Well, we know Aaron Nunamaker was killed by a bullet fired from a high powered rifle at close range. And we found this weapon near the body." Leroy wasn't sure where this was going.

"But you have no proof or evidence that this particular rifle fired the bullet that killed Aaron Nunamaker – do you?" Jack asked.

"No."

"Isn't it a fact, sheriff, since you never recovered the actual bullet that struck Aaron Nunamaker, that the killing bullet could have been fired from any similar high powered rifle? Isn't that right, sheriff?

"Yes, but..."

Jack interrupted again, "Thank you, sheriff. I have no more questions, but I do reserve the right to recall the sheriff at a later time."

"Mr. Hawks, do you have any redirect?" Judge Graves asked.

"Yes, I do Your Honor. Sheriff, did you base you assumption on this being the murder weapon because you found a spent cartridge still in the chamber of this weapon? The rifle submitted into evidence and the one belonging to Todd Randal?" Griffin asked.

"Yes sir, I did," Leroy responded with a grin.

"And has it been your experience that people do not normally leave spent cartridges in their weapons? And because one was still in the rifle, it would be your proper assumption that the rifle had been recently fired?" Griffin asked.

Jack stood up, "Objection, the question asks for a conclusion by the witness using some 'experience' not in evidence!"

Griffin looked at Judge Graves, "Your Honor! He is the sheriff!'

"Overruled," the judge said. "Sheriff, you may answer the question."

"Yes sir, that has been my experience," Leroy happily answered.

"No more questions, Your Honor," Griffin said to Judge Graves.

Jack had no re-cross questions and Leroy was excused. Griffin Hawks called his next witness, Dr. Barker Gibson County Coroner.

Dr. Barker testified that Aaron Nunamaker had died from a single gunshot wound to the chest, and specifically to the heart. He also testified that the absence of inhaled smoke in the lungs indicated that Aaron Nunamaker was dead before the fire. It was Dr. Barker's opinion that the gunshot wound had been made by a high powered rifle fired at close range, and that death was almost instantaneous. Griffin Hawks turned the witness over to Jack Logan.

Jack stood up and remained at his table. "Dr. Barker, were you able to determine the kind or caliber of weapon used to kill Aaron Nunamaker?"

"No, I was not. However, based upon the size of the entry and exit wound, my opinion is that the weapon was a high powered rifle," Dr. Barker answered.

"Can you please explain what you mean by a 'high powered rifle'?"

"Yes. I mean a rifle typically used for hunting medium or large game animals, something using 30/30 caliber ammunition or larger," Dr. Barker responded.

"But you do NOT know the caliber of bullet that killed Aaron Nunamker. Is that correct?" Jack asked again.

"That is correct. We did not find the bullet; therefore we do not know what caliber weapon was used."

"Thank you Dr. Barker." Jack then looked at Judge Graves and spoke as he sat down, "I have no further questions of this witness."

Griffin Hawks had no redirect and called his next witness, jockey Eddie Merrick.

Eddie was sworn in and testified about Todd Randal coming to the barn and his hearing loud voices that he recognized to be Aaron Nunamaker and Todd Randal. His testimony was that he could not understand what that conversation was about. Griffin Hawks then turned the witness over to Jack Logan.

"Mr. Merrick," Jack asked walking toward the witness. "What can you tell us about Mafia people removing thoroughbred horses from 'Nunamaker Stables'?"

Griffin Hawks stood up. "Objection, Your Honor – relevance."

Before Judge Graves could speak Jack said, "Your Honor, we intend to prove relevance. We intend to prove that the moving and removal of these horses was, in part, a motive for Aaron Nunamaker's murder."

Judge Graves looked at Griffin Hawks.

"Your Honor," Griffin said. "We know where the defense is trying to go with this, and it isn't relevant. This preliminary hearing is to establish that a crime has been committed and that enough evidence is present to bind the accused over for trial. The status of any horses at 'Nunamaker Stables' is simply not relevant to this case."

"Sustained," Judge Graves ruled. "Mr. Logan, you will need to find another line of questioning for this witness."

Judge Graves was not making it easy. Jack would need to try another approach.

"Okay," Jack recanted. "Mr. Merrick, isn't it true that a few days before the murder, you witnessed the trainer, Justin Avery, removing a rifle from Todd Randal's truck?"

"No sir, that is not true," Eddie responded quickly.

"Isn't it true that you witnessed Justin Avery in possession of a rifle just like the one owned by Todd Randal? If not Todd Randal's rifle, and the one submitted into evidence as the murder weapon, one just like it?" Jack asked.

"I don't know. I mean Justin has a lot of rifles; maybe he has one that looks like that one. How would I know?" Eddie was stuttering.

"And your sworn testimony is that you did not witness Justin Avery remove a rifle from Todd Randal's truck, and that you did not later witness him in possession of this weapon?" Jack was zeroing in.

"I didn't see him take any rifle from Todd's truck. I've seen him with a lot of rifles, we work on a ranch and everybody has a rifle in their truck," he seemed confused by the questions.

"Do you have a rifle in your truck, Mr. Merrick?" Jack asked.

"Yes, but it isn't like that one," he answered nervously, pointing at the burned rifle on the evidence table.

"I didn't ask you that. I asked you if you had one in your truck," Jack snapped.

"Yes," Eddie answered

"Have you checked lately to see if it is still there? Perhaps someone removed it too!" Jack questioned.

Eddie had a long pause before he answered. "I, I haven't looked lately," he stuttered.

"Thank you, Eddie." Jack spoke to Judge Graves, "Your Honor, I have no further questions for this witness."

Griffin Hawks had no redirect. Eddie Merrick was excused and Griffin was instructed to call his next witness. He called Justin Avery.

Of course, Justin Avery was still missing. Leroy was called to the bench, where he advised Judge Graves that his office had been unable to serve the subpoena because Justin could not be located. After a long sidebar, Judge Graves issued a bench warrant for Justin Avery's arrest – contempt of court. He was to be held without bond until he appeared before the court and presented acceptable reasons for his failure to respond as required.

"Mr. Hawks," Judge Graves said, "you may call your next witness."

"Your Honor, the District Attorney's office will not be calling any other witnesses for this preliminary hearing. We believe we have established that a crime has been committed and that substantial evidence is present to warrant the binding of Todd Randal over for trial. The prosecution rests," Griffin told the court.

Judge Graves looked at Jack Logan. "Mr. Logan, you may call your first witness."

"Thank you Your Honor. The defense calls Dr. Jack Preston."

Griffin Hawks stood up. "We object, Your Honor!"

Jack looked at Griffin. "What do you mean you object? You're objecting to my witness? On what grounds?"

"The same grounds as before, relevance. What did or didn't happen to those horses is simply not relevant to this case. You're trying to…"

Judge Graves interrupted them, "The last time I checked this was my courtroom, which means that your conversations need to be directed to me as the judge presiding over this hearing. I'll rule on objections and ask for arguments, if I think they are required. Do I have everyone's attention?"

"Yes sir," Jack and Griffin both answered at the same time.

"Now, Mr. Hawks, I understand your position, but the defense has the right to present evidence and call witnesses. If you don't like their questions, then you can object. But you will not object to their right to call anyone they chose. Am I clear?" Judge Graves asked Griffin directly.

"Yes sir," he responded.

"Thank you, Mr. Hawks. Your objection is overruled. Bailiff, see that the next witness, Dr. Jack Preston, is present and sworn," he said to everyone.

Technically, Leroy had arrested Dr. Jack Preston. Officially, he was being held in protective custody by the Gibson County Sheriff's office. Luckily, he was permitted to appear in court wearing civilian clothes, and not the customary orange jump suit.

Jack would need to be careful with his approach. Otherwise, Griffin Hawks would throw objections to every question and prevent him from getting to the truth.

Dr. Preston was sworn and offered his name and credentials to the court.

"Dr. Preston, how long have you practiced veterinary medicine?" Jack asked.

"32 years, almost all of it in Gibson County."

"And in your practice, were you the veterinarian of record for '*Nunamaker Stables*'?"

Griffin stood up and shouted, "Objection – relevance."

"Overruled," the judge quickly said. "Dr. Preston, you may answer the question."

"Yes, '*Nunamaker Stables*' was one of my clients," he answered.

"In your practice, do you have other thoroughbred horse breeding operations among your client list?" Jack asked.

"Yes, I have several that I work with. Most are in West Tennessee, but I have clients in Kentucky and Mississippi," he answered frankly.

"As a professional, and with your unique knowledge of how these businesses operate, would you recognize when one of your clients was running his business in an illegal or unethical manner?"

Griffin stood up and stated, "Objection – questions ask for an opinion from the witness."

Judge Graves looked at Jack.

"Sure it does," Jack said to the judge. "This man is a professional veterinarian who specializes in horse breeding operations. If we can't ask his opinion who could we ask?"

"Overruled," the judge said. "Dr. Preston, you may answer the question."

"Yes, I would quickly recognize if any of my clients were running their business in the manner that you described," he answered frankly.

"And in your professional opinion, was '*Nunamaker Stables*' running their business in an illegal or unethical manner?" Jack asked.

Griffin stood up again. "Objection, Your Honor, calls for an unqualified conclusion from the witness."

"Overruled," the judge said quickly. "Mr. Hawks, I have already ruled on this subject, so don't bring it up again! Dr. Preston, you may answer the question."

Griffin Hawks sat down in disgust. He knew where this was going and had no way to prevent it.

"Could you repeat the question?" Dr. Preston asked Jack.

"Sure. In your professional opinion, was '*Nunamaker Stables*' running their business in an illegal or unethical manner?" Jack repeated.

"Yes," he answered.

"Dr. Preston, can you give the court some examples or reasons for your opinion?"

Griffin stood up and yelled, "Objection – relevance, again."

"Sit down, Griffin!" Judge Graves snapped. "Dr. Preston, please continue."

"Certified thoroughbred breeding stock was being regularly removed from '*Nunamaker Stables*' to pay for Aaron Nunamaker's gambling debts. Uncertified animals were substituted to maintain operations. On my last visit to '*Nunamaker Stables*', only one certified thoroughbred remained in inventory - and that animal was impotent."

"Then that would mean the animals destroyed in the fire were not thoroughbred horses?" Jack asked.

"Well, I didn't see the animals. But, unless somebody brought some thoroughbreds to the fire, there was nothing more than saddle ponies and breeding mares left at '*Nunamaker Stables*'!"

The courtroom broke into laughter and Judge Graves was forced to use his gavel to silence the crowd.

"Thank you Dr. Preston. I have no more questions. Mr. Hawks, your witness," Jack offered.

"Dr. Preston," Griffin asked. "Do you know who killed Aaron Nunamaker?"

"No sir."

"Do you know if Todd Randal killed Aaron Nunamaker, or if he had a reason or motive?" Griffin asked pointedly.

"No sir. I have no knowledge of who killed Aaron Nunamaker and I don't know if Todd Randal had reason or motive. But I do know that Todd Randal would NOT have killed those horses," he answered quickly.

"Your Honor," Griffin shouted. "I move that last comment be stricken from the record! That was not a part of my question and only reflects his opinion regarding what Todd Randal would or would not do!"

The judge looked down at the District Attorney. "Griffin Hawks, you should know better than to ask a question without having some idea of the answer you will get. Request denied."

Griffin Hawks sat down frustrated and said, "I have no more questions of this witness."

"Mr. Logan, you may call your next witness," the judge offered.

"Thank you, Your Honor. The defense calls Mrs. Amanda Grayton."

When he said that, you heard a murmur go through the crowded courtroom. Griffin Hawks looked around, then shrugged his shoulders and shook his head. It seemed nobody expected Amanda Grayton to be called as a witness – nobody but Todd Randal!

Todd jumped up and yelled, "Your Honor, I am changing my plea to guilty. I did it. Amanda has no business in this courtroom and has nothing to add. I am guilty, let's get this over with!"

Judge Graves almost broke his gavel trying to calm everyone down. Once he had control, he called both Griffin Hawks and Jack Logan to the bench.

"I'll see both of you in my chambers – now!"

Then the judge told the courtroom, "This court is in a 30 minute recess. Please be back in your seats at 10:30 – sharp!"

~

In chambers Judge Graves removed his robe and looked at Jack Logan like a father with a misbehaved child.

"Okay, Jack. What is all this about?" he asked.

"It's simple, really. At some point the prosecution will introduce the idea that Todd Randal had a woman in his life and that woman was Susan Nunamaker. We have knowledge otherwise. And Amanda Grayton has been called to provide that knowledge to the court," Jack offered.

"So, it is your plan to try your case at this preliminary hearing?" the judge asked.

"It is my plan to prove to the court that Todd Randal did not kill Aaron Nunamaker. If that means trying my case and presenting my evidence, then that is what I intend to do," Jack said firmly.

"But you have the District Attorney and the Court at a disadvantage," Judge Graves admonished. "You weren't required to furnish discovery evidence or provide a witness list. We're operating in the dark, Mr. Logan, and I won't permit you to continue unless Mr. Hawks agrees."

"Your Honor," Griffin offered, "The District Attorney's office has no objection to hearing the defense witnesses. We're looking for the truth, just like the Court."

"Okay, we've cleared that hurdle," Judge Graves said to them both. "Now we've got the issue of your client changing his plea. What do you say to that, Mr. Logan?"

"I say you'll understand why he did that when you hear Amanda Grayton's testimony. You're the judge; you could simply not accept a plea change outside the course of normal court proceedings. Please understand, Your Honor, he is just upset that she has been called to testify. It in no way changes his innocence to guilt," Jack offered.

"Okay, I'll accept that. Now for the sensitive testimony, how sensitive is it?" he asked.

"You'll probably want to warn the court, it's pretty sensitive," Jack answered. "Amanda has no idea why she has been called, I don't think. And I know her husband, Billy, doesn't."

"Okay, back to court. Let's get past this as quickly as we can. Somehow I expect you, Mr. Logan, have more tricks up your sleeve!" he said to them both.

~

Judge Graves called the court back to order at 10:30 sharp. He immediately warned the court that sensitive testimony would be forthcoming and any disturbance by the audience would not be tolerated. He also informed the court that a change of plea by Mr. Todd Randal would not be accepted, at this time. He did leave the option open for Jack Logan to enter an official motion, if he desired.

Amanda Grayton was sworn and took the stand. She then identified herself by name and occupation. Billy Grayton was in the audience; he had no idea what was coming next.

"Mrs. Grayton," Jack began, "would you please tell the court where you were on the weekend of Aaron Nunamaker's murder?"

She looked shocked. "Home," was all she could manage to say.

"Can you explain why your vehicle was parked in the long-term parking garage at the Memphis airport? Why it was parked there from that Thursday through Saturday, the Saturday of Aaron Nunamakers murder?" Jack asked.

"No," she said shaking.

"Okay. Then can you explain why a one-way ticket from Memphis to Hot Springs, Arkansas was purchased and used by a Mrs. Amanda Grayton? That ticket was for travel on that Thursday, the same day your car entered the parking garage," Jack asked.

Amanda started to cry. Todd Randal stood up and yelled, "Amanda, don't answer that question."

Judge Graves cracked his gavel, "Mr. Randal, one more outburst from you and I'll have you gagged and handcuffed to your chair. Am I being clear?"

Todd sat down and hung his head.

"Your Honor, the defense has no more questions of this witness," Jack said.

Griffin Hawks stood and said, "The prosecution has no questions."

Amanda left the stand and then quickly left the courtroom. Billy Grayton had left moments earlier.

"Your Honor, the defense now calls Susan Nunamaker to the stand," Jack announced.

Susan entered the courtroom, unaware of any of the previous testimony. She was sworn and gave her name and occupation for the court.

Jack walked to the middle of the courtroom and paused before addressing the witness. "Mrs. Nunamaker, would you tell the court where you were the evening your husband was murdered?" Jack asked politely.

"I was in Hallendale Beach, Florida at Gulfstream Park racing one of my horses," she answered quickly.

"And were you with the '*Nunamaker Stables*' trainer, Justin Avery?"

"Yes, we drove down taking our trailer which contained our race horse and two riding ponies," she responded.

"Where was your personal vehicle?" Jack asked looking straight at her.

"I parked it in town. I had errands to run before we left, and Justin picked me up on his way out of town," her words were getting shaky.

"Okay, if that's true, can you explain why your vehicle was parked in the long-term parking garage of the Memphis airport? It was parked there on a Wednesday, the day you claim to have left on your drive to Florida. It was removed on that Saturday afternoon, the day your husband was murdered, and then returned to the parking garage later that night. It was then removed on Tuesday, the day you returned home to '*Nunamaker Stables*'."

"You are mistaken, I left my car parked in Humboldt," she said shaking her head.

"Okay. Can you explain why someone using the name Susan Nunamaker purchased and used a round-trip ticket from Memphis to Fort Lauderdale for travel on the same Thursday your car was reportedly left in the parking garage? And the Fort Lauderdale to Memphis portion of the ticket was for travel on the Saturday your husband was murdered?" Jack asked.

"No, you are mistaken," she said again.

"Okay. Can you explain why someone using the name Susan Nunamaker purchased and used ANOTHER round-trip ticket from Memphis to Fort Lauderdale for late night travel on the Saturday of your husband's murder and used the return portion on that following Tuesday?" Jack was looking straight at her.

"No, you are wrong. You are mistaken," she said shakily.

"Well, unfortunately Susan, I have documentation for the parking and the air travel. So, maybe you and your lawyer can figure out some story to fit the documented facts. I'm sure the sheriff will want to discuss all this with you in detail later."

"You bastard, you have made all this up to get Todd Randal off the hook," she yelled.

"No, Mrs. Nunamaker, I haven't made anything up, but let me offer my theory for your consideration and the court records," Jack added.

"Bastard," Susan mumbled.

"You and Mr. Justin Avery were a pair, a thing, and had been for a long time. That is ironic, but we won't go there now. Anyway, your husband, Aaron, had been successful in losing everything you and he had accumulated at '*Nunamaker Stables*' – either through gambling or other vices, but that doesn't matter. The Memphis Mafia had taken all your assets to pay his debts and you could see no way out. That's when you and Justin came up with this grand scheme. The insurance company doesn't know these valuable horses are no longer at '*Nunamaker Stables*', so why not burn the barn with the horses and collect insurance? With a fire, identification of the animals would be at best difficult, and most probably impossible. You're really not sure of your plan until the Mafia steals a truck and runs over one of your jockeys, that's when you realize that the whole house of cards will soon be tumbling down. At some point, Justin steals Todd's rifle and leaves it hidden in the barn, just in case. Because with your plan, you were the one who would need to do the dirty deed – burn up the horses. For your plan and alibi to work, Justin would need to be in Florida running the races. You, on the other hand as an owner, could come and go at the track without much notice.

Things got even better when you returned from Florida and found Todd and your husband in the barn having an argument about business. This was perfect and offered you a way to not only collect insurance, but to get rid of Aaron at the same time. Todd left; you retrieved Todd's rifle from where Justin had hidden it and shot your husband. Then you did the unthinkable, you brought every horse you could find and locked them up in the barn. I'm sure they followed you willingly to their ultimate death house, and why not? You were their master, their caretaker – why would you harm them?" Jack had said enough.

Jack then turned and addressed Judge Graves. "Your Honor, I move that the documents I mentioned be entered into evidence for the court and state's review. I also enter a motion that all charges against my client, Todd Randal, be dropped and he be released from custody."

Judge Graves stuck his gavel. "Mr. Hawks, do you have reasons for this hearing to continue?"

"No, your Honor," Griffin stood up and replied.

"Then I rule this hearing adjourned and I will consider all pending motions tomorrow morning. Sheriff Leroy Epsee, the court orders you to take Mrs. Susan Nunamaker into custody pending review of the evidence as presented."

Wrap Up

*T*he lunch crowd had already left Chiefs when Joe and I pulled in and parked. Jack was still at the courthouse clearing up loose ends and filing necessary paperwork. I expected Todd would be released tomorrow and he could begin picking up the pieces. A lot of lives had been changed or damaged during the past couple of weeks. I'm not certain where everyone would start putting those broken pieces back together.

Knowing Billy Grayton, he would probably be the first to forgive, if it's possible to do that. Amanda had hurt him badly and only time would determine what would happen to their relationship.

Nathan Crouch had left a message at the sheriff's office. He had all the horses loaded and was expected back in Humboldt in 2 or 3 days. That part turned out well.

Justin Avery was still on the run, but sooner or later he would turn up and join Susan Nunamaker in jail. Then he would be tried as an accessory to murder and conspiracy, not to mention his flight to avoid prosecution.

Linda Smiley had not been found, and I expected she was probably dead. The Mafia boys didn't normally leave witnesses, if they could avoid it. The good news is that the kids were being taken care of and probably getting better care than they were getting from Linda.

I figured Dr. Jack Preston was somewhere getting drunk. Leroy had let him go and it was the right thing to do. James Henry King and Johnie Gibson were in custody and in the hospital, but more importantly, they were also where they wouldn't be any trouble for Dr. Preston or anyone else. Leroy had some serious charges against both of them, and I expected it to be a while before they were back on the street.

Julio Escobar remained a loose end. He ended up with nothing and I'm sure was a very pissed off bad guy. That's never a good idea.

~

Joe and I grabbed a stool and I shouted to Nickie, "Hey beautiful, have Ronnie fix us a couple of burgers, and I'll take a Jack and Coke."

"Well, if it's not my two most famous customers. I guess court has adjourned for the day?" she asked.

"For us, it has adjourned for good. Jack did a slam dunk and Todd will walk out tomorrow a free man."

"And, who caught the bad end of this situation?" she asked while preparing my drink.

"Several people, but Susan Nunamaker will be taking the big fall. The rest of the collateral damage is pretty severe; you'll get to read about it in the Courier Chronicle. The trial was a good show, but an unhappy ending for several of your citizens," I answered.

"So, are you guys sticking around for a couple of days or headed back to the big city?" she asked us both.

"I'm headed to Tupelo to see Mom and Dad then back to Memphis," Joe responded.

"And you handsome?" she asked me.

"When I finish that hamburger and drink, I'm headed to Memphis. I have an appointment that has already been delayed too long."

"Oh, that blonde stewardess I bet," Nickie snickered.

"Maybe, but my delayed appointment is happy hour at the Starlight Lounge. If I push the Ford real hard, I can just make it!" I laughed.

~

And I did just that, windows down and enjoying the fresh air. I know I've said this before, but the air just smells better at night. All the rotten odors seem to follow the sun and leave a new freshness every evening.

I found my favorite jazz radio station and let my thoughts get tangled up in the music. A lot of lives had changed this past week and Carson Reno had been a part of those changes. I wondered why, but never questioned my involvement or intentions. Hell, I just want to make people happy. But, sometimes it just doesn't turn out that way.

Soon the music and night air made me forget the activities of the past week. Tomorrow was another day.

I was headed home, and in fact, if I tried hard enough, I think I could almost smell the Starlight Lounge!

Photo Credits

Greenranch.com

fineartamerica.com

dave-clayton.com

ponybox.com

thetrackphilosopher.com

ltc4940.blogspot.com

encyclopediaofarkansas.net

greenbutgame.org

charles-dusty.tripod.com

pickuptrucks.com

sweptline.com

myhorse.com

ehp-creative.com

history.amedd.army.mil

iwvnews.com

corbisimages.com

flickr.com

pbase.com

icles.centralkynews.com

About the Author

A Florida native, Gerald grew up in the small town of Humboldt, TN., where he attended high school. Following graduation from the Univ. of Tennessee, he spent time in Hopkinsville, KY, Memphis, TN and Newport, AR before moving back to Florida – where he now lives.

While living and working in Memphis, the author worked out of an office located just off the lobby of The Peabody Hotel. Many of the descriptions, events and stories about the hotel are from personal experiences.

This short story fiction work, "Horse Tales", is what the author calls 'Fiction for Fun'. It uses real places and real geography to spin a story that didn't happen, but should be fun for the mystery reader. As a quick read, those familiar with the 1962 geography in the novel, will travel back in time to places that will always be remembered.

This is the fourth story in the Carson Reno series. The first, "Murder in Humboldt" the second "The Price of Beauty in Strawberry Land" and third "Killer Among Us" are available in a paperback edition. His book, "Don't Wake Me Until It's Time to Go", is a non-fiction collection of stories, events and humorous observations from his life. Many friends and readers will find themselves in one of his adventures or stories.

Learn more about this author and his additional works at:

http://www.wix.com/carsonreno/carson

http://www.authorsden.com/geraldwdarnell

And

http://stores.lulu.com/geralddarnell

When visiting the web-sites, you are encouraged to leave your comments and reviews of this book and his others.

Also, please let the author know if you would like to see continuing stories with Carson Reno and his cast of characters.

You may email Carson at:

Carsonreno@msn.com

Look for Carson Reno's next adventure in:

'the

Crossing'

Scheduled to be available for the 2011 Holiday Season

"Life is Cheap – Make Sure You Buy Enough"

Carson Reno

Made in the USA
Lexington, KY
16 September 2019